imagine me

fiona cole

imagine me

© 2017 by Fiona Cole

All rights reserved.

Cover Designer: Najla Qamber, Najla Qamber Designs, www.najlaqamberdesigns.com/

Interior Design: Indie Girl Promtoions, www.IndieGirlPromotions.com/

Playlist

The Scientist – Corinne Bailey Rae
The Shell – Rose Cousins
What Kind of Man – Florence + The Machine
Hardest of Hearts – Florence + The Machine
Happy With Me – HOLYCHILD
Strip Me – Natasha Bedingfield
Standing In Front of You – Kelly Clarkson
Drumming Song – Florence + The Machine
I Don't Dance – Lee Brice
Wanted You More – Lady Antebellum
Wrecking Ball – Miley Cyrus
Road Less Traveled – Lauren Alaina
Happy – Leona Lewis
Tin Man – Miranda Lambert
Roll Away Your Stone – Mumford & Sons
Love Is Hard – James Morrison
Frist Day of My Life – Bright Eyes
Looking Out – Brandi Carlile
Pray – JRY (ft. Rooty)
...Ready For It – Taylor Swift
The Story of Us – Taylor Swift
Ask Me How I Know – Garth Brooks

To my husband.
I imagined you being there, and you were.
I love you.

Chapter One

"What if we got married?"

"Wha . . ." Shock prevented me from finishing the word.

"Marry me," Hudson said again. This time he sounded more sincere and less like he was tossing out some ludicrous idea at random. "Then you can come back home and stop this charade in Cincinnati."

My eyes widened as my confusion mixed with anger. *Charade?* "We haven't been together in over a year." My voice was shrill, and I struggled to keep it low as we stood among the throng of people trying to check their bags and head to their gates. "Besides, you don't even have a ring."

"Come on, Jules. We've been best friends forever." *Best* friend was an exaggeration. "Our families are close and it makes sense that we'd end up together. We fit. I'd never imagined having anyone else by my side."

"But you've seen other people since we separated. It's not like you've been pining over me and trying to get me back." It had seemed to me he had been almost relieved to get the chance to date other women since we'd split up. My nose scrunched. His surprise proposal had scattered all my thoughts.

"Yeah, but I always assumed we'd end up married. I figured you just needed some space so you can feel like you've lived a little before we settled down."

Before I became the perfect Southern belle and married the man who was supposed to take over my father's company? Hudson had never taken anyone else to one of my family's charity fundraisers because it would've been insulting to take a date when it was assumed that I'd eventually be Mrs. Hudson Murphy.

My mouth hung open as I struggled to come up with words to make him understand. It turned out he didn't need a response from me to keep on talking.

"I mean, what more do you want? Your parents let you go to college. They even let you go to grad school. And how do you repay them? By not coming home after you graduate. Think about it."

A dull roar echoed inside my head. "They let me?" I asked incredulously. "I'm an adult."

"You're the baby of the family."

"That doesn't mean I deserve any less." My face heated with frustration for having to defend my right to be my own person. "I thought you understood me. How many conversations did we have where I bared my secrets to you? How many times did I tell you I wanted more than to be a society wife?"

He shrugged as if I were simply being difficult. As if he weren't actually insulting me. "I figured it was a phase. One you needed to explore on your own while you still had time in grad school. So, yes. I was supportive and didn't say anything. Didn't put up a fight and let you have your space because I loved you, and I wanted you to get it out of your system. I figured you had an itch you needed to explore, but to be honest, after your trip to Jamaica, it seemed to get worse."

I ignored the comment about Jamaica, not wanting to explain the things that trip had made me want to explore. He had no idea I had met a man there who had lit a fire in me greater than any Hudson could have hoped to kindle. Instead, I focused on his silence when he could've told me how he felt a year ago.

Not that it would have made any difference.

"You didn't say a word when I explained my plan to go to Cincinnati and stay with Jack. I thought you supported me."

"I didn't actually think you'd follow your brother to another state when your dad threatened to pull all financial support. I figured you'd come to your senses at some point."

"Come to my senses," I muttered heatedly.

"I know how stubborn you are, Jules." He said it softly, like he was trying to remind me how well he knew me. Yet there he stood, baffled that I wasn't tossing aside my future, my hopes and dreams, to fulfill the role expected of me by my parents. "If I'd have let you see how frustrated you were making me, you'd have dug your heels in further."

Screaming would probably send the TSA running from all directions, yet that was exactly what I wanted to do. "I wasn't some stubborn child, Hudson, throwing a fit."

He cocked an eyebrow at me like I was exactly that, a stubborn child. I had to keep myself from stomping my foot. If he thought I was throwing a tantrum now, then I'd happily show him how bad a tantrum I could throw.

"And now you're living in Cincinnati with an unsafe car. What other risks are you willing to take for this so-called independence?"

He used air quotes around independence and I wanted to slap his stupid fingers down. And how dare he insult Betsy, my old Honda Civic. She wasn't always the most dependable, but she was all mine. I'd been proud of myself when I'd come home at

Thanksgiving to share the news. My father had grumbled how I was putting myself in jeopardy, and Hudson had watched me with a clenched jaw.

His tone softened, but his words still let me know how little he cared about what I wanted. "You're twenty-five, Jules. How much longer are you going to keep up this nonsense? Most women your age are already settled down with a husband and are thinking about kids."

I couldn't believe this was happening. "You don't know me at all." The frustration I felt had me practically growling.

"Juliana." He sighed my name and ran a hand through his hair.

"And it's not nonsense." I jabbed a finger in his face, and with that parting reminder, I turned to storm away. I was immediately stopped by his strong fingers circling my thin wrist.

"Don't leave like this," he pleaded. He looked at me with truly soft eyes. "I'm sorry I threw that out there. It was wrong of me."

He looked at me like the friend I grew up with. The one who understood me and never liked arguing with me. But I wasn't ready to let him off the hook just yet. "Damn right it was."

"You're my friend, always have been." He spoke softer and moved his hand down my wrist, wrapping it around my fingers. "Always will be."

"Then what is this all about?" For the life of me, I couldn't figure how we got from him walking me into the airport, to asking me to marry him right before I entered the TSA checkpoint.

He ran a hand through his dark hair and tugged. "I don't know, Jules. I guess I didn't expect you to leave. And then when you did, I assumed you'd decide to come back before too long. I figured maybe you were waiting for something to ground you here, and if I threw it out there, you could come home."

"I'm not some rebellious teenager trying to stick it to my family. Like you said, I'm twenty-five. And rather than seeing it as a point to settle down, I see it as a time to live. To explore." I stretched my arms wide and shook my head. "I get that I'm the baby, and a girl, but at some point, I have to be allowed to live my own life."

He rolled his lips across his teeth, assessing me. "Have you even looked for an apartment yet? Or are you going to live with your brother and his wife indefinitely?" His tone was laced with skepticism.

"Yes, I'm looking," I answered primly, chin held high.

He sighed and pinched his lips before asking his other question, the one he already knew the answer too. "And your car?"

"Betsy and I are just fine, thank you very much."

"Juliana."

"Hudson." I dropped my arms to my sides and relaxed my stance. "I'm looking for an apartment, but I want to make it worth it. And I will get a better car once I have more in savings. I just started my job in September, so I need time to build a nest egg. My parents taught me well about managing money, and now I need to be able to apply it." I needed to get to my gate soon, and I didn't want to leave on a sour note. I made a joke like we always used to do before all this tension.

"I thank you for your extravagant proposal. You were so many of my firsts, so it only seems fair that you would be the first person to ask me to marry him."

"Next time it will be better. With a ring." His tone didn't hold nearly as much humor as I expected. It sounded more like a promise. "I'm always here, Jules. And I'll be waiting for when you're ready to come home."

"Don't wait for me, Hudson."

He didn't answer, just gave me a sad smile and pulled me in for a hug. I wrapped my arms around his waist and breathed in his familiar spicy scent—Dolce & Gabbana *Light Blue*.

"Thanks for bringing me to the airport," I mumbled into his chest. "I should be back for Easter."

"Anytime. Let me know when you land." With that he placed a soft kiss against my hair, pulled back, and waved goodbye before disappearing into the crowd.

I grabbed my bag off the conveyor belt almost thirty minutes earlier than scheduled. I'd messaged Evie, my sister-in-law's best friend, and she'd let me know she'd be there. My brother was supposed to have picked me up, but he'd bailed and sent Evie in his place. As long as I didn't have to pay for a long Uber ride home, I was fine.

The doors slid open and a cold blast of air hit me, so different from the Texas heat that never seemed to lessen. I scanned down the row of cars looking for my Evie's little red MINI Cooper.

But before I could find it, my attention was diverted to a mess of dark curls swirling in the wind attached to a petite body. I almost decided the cost of an Uber would be worth it when I read the sign Evie waved at me.

Model MacCabe

Welcome home from jail.

"Juliana MacCabe, I've missed you so much." She shouted from ten feet away. "You look so good. That prison food must be better than I assumed."

People turned to stare, and I wished I was shorter than my five-foot-ten self so I could hide among the crowd. Heat burned up my cheeks and I marched toward her, if for no other reason than to make her stop yelling.

"Really, Evelyn?"

"What?" She smiled innocently, glancing at the sign. "You do look like a model with your sharp cheekbones and runway-ready body. And you've mentioned how being home with your parents can sometimes feel like jail. I don't see what's so wrong with the sign."

She was so honest about it, I just had to laugh. She bobbed her eyebrows and smirked, knowing she'd won.

"Where's your car? I'm ready to go home. And what happened to Jack?"

"He said something came up." She shrugged and popped her trunk.

I loaded my suitcase and we got on our way. Evie glanced over at me.

"Rough trip home?"

I breathed a laugh at how much of an understatement that was. It's not like it was a bad trip. Jack and Luella had been there for a couple of days, which helped distract my parents, but the rest of the time, they looked at me like I was an errant teenager on the verge of mental breakdown. I got it, I was the baby. I arrived ten years after Jack, blessing in disguise, and they coddled me from day one. Don't get me wrong, I love my family fiercely, but I needed space to grow and find out who I was.

My hastened desire to leave Texas and rush to Cincinnati had nothing to do with the passionate night I'd had in Jamaica. It had nothing to do with my brother's friend, Shane, sparking a need in me I hadn't known existed. One I doubted I would ever find again if I stayed in Texas. It had nothing to do with the fact that Shane lived in Cincinnati and I imagined the possibility of hooking up with him again.

Nope. Not. At. All.

"Can I ask you something?" I asked, sidestepping her question. At her nod, I continued. "You used to be independent, right?"

Evie scoffed. "Bitch, I'm still independent. I just now have a sexy as sin man by my side."

"Fair enough." I raised my hands in defeat. Taking a deep breath, I decided to share what had happened with Evie. "My ex-boyfriend asked me to marry him before I took off."

Her eyebrows shot upward and her eyes shifted to look at my hand. "And? I don't see a ring on your finger."

"He would've had to have a ring for that to happen."

"The man proposed without a damn ring? Hell no." She shook her head and pursed her lips in disappointment.

"He proposed without a plan. I'm pretty sure without even thinking it through."

"And you said no. Good for you." She watched me pick at my chipped nail polish. "I feel like there is more to this. Start from the top."

"Ha." I barked out a laugh. "I don't know. We dated for a long time, and we've known each other forever, but I broke up with him a little over a year ago because I needed to explore. Once I was in grad school, I knew I wasn't planning on staying in Texas. I wanted to be able to leave without having him waiting for me. I wanted to find out who I am on my own. He's always been my friend, and I'd assumed he'd supported me. Turns out he's been in line with my parents in thinking I should come home." I stopped picking at my nails and twisted my fingers on my lap. "But I want to *live,* Evie. I don't want to only be known as some rich man's wife. I want to explore. Explore the world, myself, my sexuality."

She remained quiet, and I worried that I'd said too much and made her uncomfortable. It felt impossible to do with Evie, but you never know.

"First things first. You do you. Period. And to do that, you need to move out of your brother's house. Because he's still there and we all know how protective Jack can be when it comes to you. There will be no drunken nights of stupid ideas and one night stands around him."

"I'm surprised he doesn't have an ankle tracker on me." We both laughed at how true that statement was. Jack ran his own security company, and had plenty of access to all those gadgets to keep me from exploring too far. He knew I hadn't wanted the life my parents expected of me. He'd been understanding of that, but it hadn't stopped him from forever seeing me as a baby who constantly needed protecting.

"Once you move out, then you can be as free as you want. Drink all the alcohol, throw parties, drive around in your shit car without hearing about it every morning. Have all the sex with all the men—just use condoms. The possibilities are endless."

Sex. I was surprised I hadn't forgotten what that was, it had been so long. About eight months to be exact. I hadn't stayed celibate on purpose. It was just that the last time I'd had sex, the bar had been set so damn high, I was scared to jump with anyone else. And being in the same city as the man who'd set that bar, I couldn't deny hoping to see him again and maybe have another go.

Another go of his rough hands on me as they held my legs apart. Another go of him wrapping his body around me from behind as he bit my shoulder and moaned his release against me.

Yeah, I needed my own place. If I ever got another chance, I'd need somewhere to take him.

We pulled up to my temporary home. It was actually my sister-in-law, Luella's family home. Jack moved in when they got together. It was pretty big, especially by downtown standards, and they were letting me stay until I found a place of my own.

I inserted my key and opened the door.

"Yes. Yes." Luella's chanted words greeted me and Evie as we stepped through the front door.

My brother's bare ass peeking out of his jeans as he flexed and pushed into Luella was the first thing I saw when I jerked my head in the direction of the living room.

I dropped the handle of my suitcase and covered my eyes, letting out a horrified yelp of disgust. I jerked in the direction of the door and bolted, completely judging the distance wrong and ran into the door itself, bouncing back, almost falling. "Fuck. Ouch." I peeked past my hands and shoved past a laughing Evie to get out.

"Nice ass, MacCabe," Evie said.

"Get out, Evelyn," my brother's voice bellowed from the open door.

She lifted her hands in defeat and stepped out.

"I guess something really did come up," Evie muttered, still smiling.

I shuddered, wishing I could bleach my mind of the last five minutes.

Yeah, moving out had just jumped to the top of my priority list.

Chapter Two

"Hey, girl, hey." My lab mate, Jolene, spun her chair in circles giving me the wink and the gun. I laughed as she slowed to a stop and turned to face me as I settled in at my desk in the lab. It was good to see her. I'd been home for a week and was ready to get back into the pattern. "How were the holidays?"

My body sagged into my chair with an exasperated sigh. "Good. Nothing like sitting around the tree on Christmas morning and defending your decision to be in Cincinnati. Merry Christmas to me." My fingers waggled, giving jazz hands and a fake smile.

"Hey. Me too." Jolene sat up excitedly in her chair, but it didn't take long to pick on her sarcasm. "Because fuck, the six years I slaved away at school and all the research awards I won. Science is nothing for a pretty little girl like me. I should just move back home and marry a good man. Be a good little wife."

"You don't sound bitter at all."

She shrugged. "Not even a little bit."

I laughed and hit the button to bring my computer to life. "If it makes you feel any better, I was welcomed home to my brother's ass as he fucked my sister-in-law against the living room wall. My efforts to move have increased ten-fold."

Jolene's jaw dropped before she threw her head back and cackled. I glowered.

"You're right. That does make me feel better. Especially imagining your brother's tight ass. Mm mm." Her eyebrows bobbed up and down.

"Gross, Jolene."

"Well today is your lucky day, chica." She spun in her chair again, arms held wide. "My roommate got engaged on Christmas." Her eyes rolled. "Cheesy, I know—but she's moving out."

Tiny waves of excitement shot through me, though I tried to ignore them until I knew for sure she was serious. "It's not funny to play with my emotions, Jo."

"Why would I play with your emotions when I'm still busy imagining your brother's naked ass?"

I threw a paper clip at her. "Stop it."

"Juliana." Dr. Stahl's voice boomed across the lab, announcing his presence.

"If it isn't Mr. Misogyny," Jolene muttered under her breath.

"Dr. Voet wants to see you in his office. Jolene, I'd like to double-check your procedures. Make sure you're doing them correctly." He didn't look up from his iPad as he barked orders at us before turning to leave again. Jolene rolled her eyes and pretended to shoot herself in the head.

Dr. Stahl was the biochemistry professor at the University of Cincinnati and ran the lab where we worked. He was Russian with a strong accent that made his orders sound harsher than most. He also had horrible manners, but worst of all were his beliefs about women in science. Yet, Jolene and I were the two lucky women to keep the lab going as his senior research associates and teaching assistants. Someday, I hoped to go back to school for my Ph.D. and have a lab of my own. Until then, Jolene and I worked like a well-oiled machine, dodging Dr. Stahl's jaundiced eye as much as possible.

I ducked out of the lab and headed to Dr. Voet's office. He was the dean of the chemistry department and also a professor in inorganic chemistry. I shook out my limbs before knocking on the door. The man was freaking gorgeous, and I always got a little nervous when I was around him. He may have been the hottest scientist I'd ever seen, with his dark, scruffy beard and longish hair that he was always pushing back off his head. And boy did I love it when a piece flopped forward. His biceps would flex as he threaded his fingers into his hair and shoved it back, all the way down to where it brushed against his collar.

I will not blush. I will not stare.

My knuckles sounded too loud against the door in the empty office. It was before eight, so his secretary wasn't in yet.

"Come in," his slightly accented voice called out. Jolene gushed over the faint lilt in his speech. She Googled him and discovered he was Dutch. I didn't know what they put in the water over there, but they did right with Dr. Voet. It didn't hurt that he was actually friendly and treated all the employees in the department equally.

I pushed the door open. "Dr. Stahl said you wanted to see me?"

"Yes, come in. Have a seat." He stood by a shelf that held a Keurig and some cups and gestured to the seats in front of his desk with a warm smile. "Can I get you a coffee? I know it's early."

"No. Thank you though. I had one on the way in and too much caffeine will ruin my steady hand."

"We wouldn't want that." He sat and brought his mug to his smiling lips. Before taking a sip, he mumbled, "Wouldn't want to make Dr. Stahl any angrier than he is."

A laugh escaped at his unexpected joke. It was no secret that Dr. Stahl was the Grinch of the department. It just caught me off guard when our dean made a joke about one of his staff. I laughed a little harder when I saw what his mug said.

Lab Rule #3. If you don't know what you're doing, at least do it neatly.

"Nice mug."

He shifted it in his hands and looked at the front. "It's a good rule."

"I'll keep it in mind."

He took one last sip, and eyed me over the rim. *Don't stare. Don't blush.* I managed to look away, waiting for him to speak first.

"Anyway, Ms. MacCabe. I called you in here because I have a job that I think you would be perfect for, considering the lab you worked in while attaining your master's degree." I raised my eyebrows and waited for him to explain. "I'd like for you to train the new forensic toxicologists and technicians in the Cincinnati Police Department's Forensic Unit."

A tingling started low in my abdomen and fluttered up through my chest at hearing the possibility of going to the police department. I knew a certain detective there and just the thought of possibly seeing him, of having a reason to stop and talk to him, made my breath catch. My imagination sparked at the thought of running into him in the hallway at the department and him tugging me into the bathroom to pick up where we left off in Jamaica.

"They're taking on more employees and need help training them on the equipment and techniques," Dr. Voet continued, completely unaware of the bells and whistles taking up residence inside me. "I know we've discussed the experience you have with the instruments, and I thought you'd be a perfect fit. You would head to the department lab twice a week instead of being Dr. Stahl's TA."

"Does that mean Jolene will be his sole TA?" My face scrunched up at the idea of leaving poor Jo taking the brunt of Dr. Stahl's rudeness.

"No." Dr. Voet chuckled at my expression. "We'll have a student from the master's program help this semester."

"Well, then. Wow." I didn't know what else to say. I was blown away by the opportunity to work so independently. "Thank you."

"Of course. I see how well you work as a teaching assistant and I thought, with your patience and the way you take the time to explain things, that you'd be perfect."

"Well, thank you."

He returned my smile as I stood, and we agreed to meet again and talk before I was needed at the department in a few weeks.

I had a little more pep in my step as I skipped into the lab and sat at my bench. Jolene stared at me with a pinched expression on her face.

"What?"

"No one is allowed to be that happy in this lab. Spill the beans."

After I explained my meeting with Dr. Voet to Jolene, she rolled over to slap my arm. "You lucky bitch."

"I know." I agreed easily as I plucked out two blue nitrile gloves.

Jolene cocked her head to the side. "Didn't you say you knew someone who worked as a detective in the CPD?"

I focused on fitting my hands in the gloves and thought about how to answer. Did I know him? Not really. But I knew what he tasted like. I knew the sound he made when he came. I knew how rough his hands felt as they palmed my breasts and pinched my nipples.

"What's that blush for?" Jolene asked with narrowed eyes.

"Nothing." I turned in my chair and grabbed my notebook, hoping she would drop it.

No such luck.

"Unh-uh, Juliana MacCabe. I need details."

I turned to face her, rolling my eyes. "I don't really know anyone. But I may have slept with someone that works there when I was in Jamaica for my brother's wedding."

Jolene's smile was big and knowing. "This is the guy your brother sometimes works with isn't it. Shane?"

I didn't respond. Just pinched my lips and stared at the wall over her shoulder.

"Ooooo. This is going to be great." She clapped her hands and rubbed them together as though plotting a trap. "When is the last time you saw him? Do you still talk to him? Maybe you can continue the hook-up now that he's so convenient. Maybe he can use his handcuffs this time."

"Oh, enough," I interrupted. "I haven't spoken to him since that night. I've actually only seen him when we've crossed paths at my brother's office. On those rare occasions, I say hello, and he responds with a head nod as he bolts out the door." I hated those times. Especially at first. I remembered the first time, walking in and seeing his broad back not long after moving to Cincinnati. I'd been swinging by to have lunch with Jack and Shane had stood, leaning against Jack's office door. My heart beat in double time and my body heated, remembering the way he'd worked me over. What would I say? Would his eyes simmer across my skin? Would he smile, and demand I have dinner with him so we could repeat that night? Would he look at me with regret and apologize for abandoning me in the early rise of the morning?

None of those things happened. He'd briefly glanced in my direction before nodding and leaving. He'd barely looked at me, and there was no recognition in his eyes. They had been blank. It had been the biggest shock for him to treat me like that, and the few times we'd crossed paths since then, it had been the same thing.

"He probably isn't even in the building where the lab is. You know there are different department buildings."

"Maybe he won't. But maybe he will," Jolene said, her eyes flashing in excitement.

I shrugged, trying to tamp down the butterflies that had taken flight in my stomach at the thought of being around him long enough for him to actually look at me and acknowledge me.

"Well, either way, I want all the details." Jolene tugged her goggles back on her face. "And since you'll be my roommate, you won't be able to escape me."

I rolled my eyes at her chipper tone and assumption that I'd move in. I mean, I was, but she could've at least waited for me to say yes. Laughing to myself, I tugged my own goggles down to get to work. Before I got too far, my phone vibrated on the bench next to me.

Hudson: I hope you made it home okay. You never checked in. Have you found an apartment yet? If not, you are always welcome home.

That was one hell of a loaded text. I couldn't wait to rub in his face that, as a matter of fact, I had found an apartment. He would learn, along with the rest of my family, that Cincinnati was my new home, and I was just fine on my own.

Chapter Three

"Finally done with the last of my clothes. Only four-thousand, three-hundred, and seventy-six more boxes to go."

"Don't exaggerate. That room will only hold four-thousand, three-hundred boxes." Jolene leaned against the kitchen counter, playfully rolling her eyes as she licked the ice cream off her spoon.

I placed my hands on my hips and nodded. "You're right. I'm a total drama queen."

"I may have to kick you out if you don't get it together." She pointed her spoon at me as I walked into the kitchen where I snagged my own spoon and dug into the mint chocolate chip.

"Then who would buy you ice cream on the second day of living here?"

"Fine. I'll let you stay a little longer." She tapped my spoon with hers while I laughed.

Jack, two of his employees, and Jack's brother-in-law, Jameson, helped move me in yesterday. Between the four of them and my minimal belongings, it only took one trip. They made it seem so easy, but there was nothing easy about unpacking boxes all day. But it was worth it. Jolene's apartment was newer, with an open layout and two bedrooms and bathrooms. The bedrooms were both the same size, except the master had an en suite.

The real bonus was never, ever, walking in on my brother and his wife again. I mentally shuddered at the slightest reminder.

My phone vibrated against the granite countertop, and I abandoned my spoon to read the message from my sister-in-law.

Luella: Come over for grilling. Everyone's coming.
Luella: Bring Jolene.

Everyone.
Did that include Shane?

I liked to play this game with myself. I figured a lot of people did, at least that's what I told myself to rationalize my overactive imagination. I would think of these extravagant situations that would never happen, but I'd let them play out in my mind and let my heart rate speed up like they would actually come to fruition.

I'd been in Cincinnati six months and hadn't had one let's-sit-down-and-chat kind of run-in with Shane, but it didn't stop me from imagining. Yesterday I waited impatiently at Jack's for everyone to show up to help move, hoping maybe he would've been one of the guys Jack called to help. Maybe we would've exchanged heated glances when no one was looking, and afterward, he would stay to help me unpack . . . And undress.

For the first few months whenever driving around Cincinnati, I looked at every police car, not that a detective would be driving a police car, and wondered if it would be him. Maybe he'd pull me over for speeding and demand sex to get out of the ticket. So many possibilities. I knew my little daydreams were crazy, but my body failed to pick up on that, what with the way it heated and tingled in preparation for a man that never came.

Like it did now, letting the chance that Shane may be part of the "everyone" Lu mentioned. My skin warmed and my heart skipped a beat. Maybe he'd wait for me to leave Jack's and follow me home, where he would knock on the door and ravish me as soon as I opened it.

Probably not though.

"That was Lu," I said to Jo. "They're cooking out and want us to head over. You game?"

"Free food? Hell yes."

When we pulled up, the driveway was almost full and all the lights were on. We got out and were greeted with the smell of burgers on the grill wafting from the backyard. Winter be damned. Nothing was going to stop Jack from using his grill. He loved that damn thing.

"They can be a little rowdy, but everyone is pretty awesome." I went to go open the door, but stopped and gave Jolene one last warning. "Beware of Evie. Super awesome. Super bold. Try to hide your fear."

With that I pushed the door open. No one was in the front room where the stereo was playing some jazz music my brother favored. I hung our coats on the rack by the door and led the way to the voices in the kitchen.

"Juliana." Luella greeted me with open arms and pulled me in for a hug. "I'm so glad you could make it. Dinner's almost ready. Evie," she directed over her shoulder. "Take them into the dining room and introduce everyone."

"You got it, boss." Evie saluted Lu with a glass of wine and led the way.

Walking in I saw all the guys standing around. I recognized one from Jack's office, then there was Jameson, Jack, and—.

If my imagination could conjure up a faster heartbeat and rapidly warming skin, then the real thing was setting my heart off at a gallop and my skin heated like a wildfire.

Shane.

He stood leaning against the table, legs cross at the ankles. He held a beer bottle in his hand and was laughing at something Jameson had said. Blood pounded through my veins and sent a whooshing sound in my ears.

"Boys, you all know Jack's sister, Juliana. And this is her friend . . ." Evie faded off waiting for Jo to fill in her name.

"Jolene," she said with a small wave. "Thanks for having me."

"Jolene?" The guy I didn't know repeated.

"Yup. Puerto Rican parents who really loved Dolly Parton."

"I love it," Evie said. "Well, since you're new let me introduce everyone."

"I'm Evie. You've already met Lu, Jack and Jameson." She pointed off each guy in the room, landing on the tall blonde in the back. "This is Clark, he works for Jack. And this big, silent one is Shane."

Shane slanted a small smile Jo's way with a head nod before his eyes moved to me. I fully expected them to flick away like usual, but this time they lingered. His jaw ticked and nostrils flared, but then he looked away and drained his bottle. It was the first time he'd actually *seen* me. It was the first time he gave any sign that he remembered me.

There was no stopping the smile slowly stretching my lips. Maybe tonight would turn out somewhat like I'd imagined. My hopeful heart soared at the merest idea.

"Hey, Jules." Jack came over and kissed my cheek. "Jolene. I'm glad you could come."

"Thanks for the invite."

"Make yourselves at home. There's beer and wine in the fridge. I'm about done at the grill. Shane, come help me bring the food in."

Shane's eyes flicked to mine one last time before turning to follow Jack out. When I went to follow Evie back into the kitchen, I was met with Jolene's wide, knowing eyes that shifted to the doors outside. I shrugged, playing ignorance about her acknowledging Shane, and walked into the kitchen.

We each got a glass of wine and stood around as Lu finished putting together the salad. I almost choked on my drink when Evie asked, "Is that the first time you've seen Shane since the wedding?" There was a glint in her eye, and I did my best to banish the red creeping into my cheeks.

Looking into my glass, I responded, "Yeah. Why?"

She waited for me to look up at her before she cocked an eyebrow. "No reason." She held my eyes. "He doesn't come around much. Too much of a loner and very private."

"He has beer with the guys every once in a while," Lu chimed in. "He's actually pretty close to Jack. An anomaly according to Jack, because he said Shane's not really close to anyone."

"Hmm. Maybe he's looking to change that."

"What makes you say that?" Lu asked.

No matter how much I tried to avoid Evie's eyes, I kept looking back. She knew. I didn't know how she knew, but she did. The silence became more apparent when Jolene cleared her throat uncomfortably.

"What?" Lu asked, looking at everyone. She stared between me and Evie, and it didn't take long to click. "No. No, no, no." She faced me. "Jack would lose his mind if he found out you liked Shane. Juliana, he's a perpetually single guy. I've never seen him with the same woman twice, and I always hear about his exploits."

"It's nothing." I waved my hand and tried to control the high pitched panic in my voice. "Don't tell Jack anything. Evie is just assuming too much. It's nothing."

Evie scoffed, but thankfully remained silent, and Lu looked unconvinced.

"Other than he's hot." Jo inserted her opinion. "Anyone can appreciate that mountain-sized body and those ice-blue eyes. Nnng," she groaned. "And that scruff."

"Do you need a minute?" Evie laughed.

Jolene took a deep breath and pursed her lips in thought. "Nah, I'm good."

Her joke broke the tension and we all laughed. Each of us grabbed a dish and took it to the table where the guys were already waiting with the meat. Praise everything good and holy, because there was an open seat by Shane and since Jo sat by Clark, it was the only place left.

Thank god for all the conversation to drown out my heartbeat. It vibrated in my chest, and I was sure if the room was quiet, everyone would be able to hear it. The whole time, I was acutely aware of Shane next to me. I hadn't been this close to him in almost a year. I wondered if he was just as excited as me. If he was having a hard time focusing on the conversation because he was remembering our night in Jamaica.

"You think you can sneak into my room, put these perky tits in my face and not expect me to suck on them?" His tongue traveled down my breastbone, parting my satin robe. Kneeling between my spread legs, he stared down at me, taking in my bare body. "I'm going to do so much more than taste your breasts. I'm going to eat your cunt. Listen to you scream and beg me to let you orgasm. I'm going to pinch your rosy nipples and lick up all that cum. Make you all nice and wet, so I can fuck you as hard as I want." He leaned over me, nibbling at my trembling lips, pressing his cock to my core. "You made a mistake sneaking in here, little girl, but since you're here, I'm going to use you up."

I had to clench my fists around the silverware to help stop the shaking. Once I had it under control, I reached out to take a drink of water, hoping to cool myself down.

Toying with my fraying nerves, Jolene kept shooting me looks, and waggling her eyebrows. I almost choked on a bite of cheeseburger when she ate her hot dog a little inappropriately.

"You okay over there?" Jack asked, concerned.

"Yup." I leveled a death stare over at Jolene who shrugged innocently.

"Gag reflex giving you trouble?" Shane's voice rumbled across my skin. It was the first thing he'd said to me all night. The first thing he'd said to me at all in nine months. And it was laced with a lot more meaning than a simple question. I turned to look at him for the first time since I sat down, and one side of his lips had barely curved up. It was the knowing glint in his eye that sent a blush roaring into my cheeks. A look that said he knew how good my gag reflex was. He'd tested it well that night.

"Watch it, Shane. That's my little sister you're joking about." Jack's voice was light as he pointed his fork at Shane. Like he didn't think he had to be serious enough to actually worry about Shane flirting with me.

Shane looked at Jack and his lips tipped more firmly in a smirk that was meant to taunt him. "C'mon, man. I think she can handle all I've got going on." My skin prickled when he dragged his finger along my shoulder, firing Jack up. My chest heaved from nerves and from having him touch me again. Even if it was a faint graze along three inches of my body through my sweater. Even if he did jerk away like he'd been burned from the small connection.

Jack, still playful, cocked his brow at Shane. "The real question is can you handle life without your balls if you even think about my sister that way."

"Jack," I interrupted, not wanting to be spoken about like I was some child.

"Juliana," he said, staring innocently at me. He used to be the overprotective brother all through high school, but I wasn't fifteen anymore.

"I don't think many men would be able to handle Juliana," Evie cut in between the sibling stare down. "I bet she'll crush all the men of Cincinnati. I'll be sure to help her." She gave me a nod of solidarity.

"Ha. Ha." Jack was not amused, as all the girls clinked glasses. Shane turned back to his meal.

The conversation moved on after that, until we all finished and began clearing the table. The night was coming to a close and the pressure increased in my chest as my chances of talking to Shane alone became more and more limited. So, when I saw him head off to the bathroom, I followed.

When he came out, he looked at me leaning against the wall. The hallway was narrow and away from everyone else, so we were left with a little privacy.

"Hey." I stood up and took a step closer.

"Hi." His eyes flicked down each end of the hallway, checking to see if anyone was watching, then back to me. I tried to see something in his face, something in the depths of his blue eyes. Anything that would give me an inkling that I was making the right move. But they remained mostly blank, other than a tinge of caution. Fuck it. I had to take this chance.

"So . . ." My voice came out a little high-pitched and I cleared my throat. I wanted to sound confident and seductive, not like Minnie Mouse. "I was thinking, maybe you can come by tonight. Or whenever you're not busy." I wanted him to know the offer was open past tonight.

I watched for a reaction and my breath caught when I saw a spark in his eyes, but it faded too quickly for me to decipher. The silence stretched for hours, each passing second making me more nervous. His jaw clenched and he swallowed, looking over toward the family room where everyone was hanging out.

When he looked back at me, his eyes were no longer blank, but hard.

"No, Mini MacCabe." His tone was condescending, as if he were speaking to a child, and it was the first hit to my confidence. "I work with your brother and just because you caught me off guard that night, doesn't mean I'll make the same mistake again."

Mistake? Mistake? The word rolled over me, crushing my lungs under the weight of what it meant. *I was a mistake?*

"You're cute, and you're a good fuck, but I'm much too old for you. Find some little boy your own age to play with." And with that, he left me alone in the hallway.

My eyes burned, and I looked away, because hell no was I going to cry. My mind scrambled at how quickly my imagination had crumbled. This was not how I'd expected the conversation to go. He may as well have patted me on the head when he delivered his speech.

I was cute?

Find some little boy my own age?

I was a mistake?

My pain morphed with each line replaying in my head and shifted to anger.

Good fuck?

He was full of shit. That night was amazing and if I was such a mistake, maybe he shouldn't have repeated it three more times that night. I could still hear his moans replaying in my mind, reminding me of just how much he enjoyed himself.

Fuck him.

My anger took over my imagination. The possibilities changing. Plans began forming.

I'd find a *man*. A man better than him and then I'd rub it in his face. I'd take Evie's advice and crush all the weak men of Cincinnati until I could find one that made Shane look like a little boy.

That asshole was going to regret calling me a mistake.

Chapter Four

"You can do this. Shane won't be in there. He's probably in another district." I squeezed my hands around the steering wheel, my knuckles turning white, and continued with my pep talk as I sat in the parking lot outside the station. "And if he is in there, you won't even see him. You'll be locked away in a lab he'll have no business being in. Hell, he may not even be in the building. Probably roaming the streets as a super cop anyway. You can do this."

I squeezed my eyes shut and took a deep breath to further steady myself. But behind my closed lids, I imagined walking in and seeing him. He would stare at me and realize what an ass he was, and what a huge mistake he'd made. He'd eye me across the room and follow me to the lab, where he'd sweep all the pipette tips off the counter and take me right there.

"Enough," I growled. I needed to shut down my imagination and get in there. I didn't want to be late on my first day.

I entered the one-story brick building and was checked-in. Security at the entrance looked through my purse and had me walk through a metal detector. While all of this went on, they made a phone call and by the time I had my jewelry back on, a dark-skinned woman with curls that bounced with each step, strode toward me.

"Juliana?" she asked with a smile.

"That would be me." I moved my purse to the crook of my arm and offered an awkward wave.

"How nice to meet you." She took my floundering hand and shook it. "I'm Laney, supervisor of the crime scene unit. I'll be showing you around and helping you get settled."

I followed her down a labyrinth of hallways as she pointed out things here and there until she opened a set of double doors to the lab. "And this is where you will be most of the time."

"Oh, wow." I stroked my fingers lovingly across the new science equipment, the large machines unmarred by years of wear and tear. "Is this the new RapidFire Mass Spectrometer? It's so beautiful."

"Spoken like a true lab rat." She laughed softly at the way I looked at each instrument with reverence. "We recently got funding to upgrade some of our space and old equipment. And with more space, we can hire more people. That's where you come in. We've worked closely with Dr. Voet and the entire department at UC. We believe in hiring locally as much as possible and helping each other out. So, thank you for taking the time to come here."

"I was honored to be chosen. This is one hell of an experience."

She walked me around the lab, explaining how it was set up and introduced me to some of the workers there. I got a good vibe from the space and my excitement increased.

"Why don't I show you the rest of the building? Get you comfortable with your surroundings should you need to go anywhere else."

I set my purse down at my bench and followed her, trying to remember each turn we took so I could find my way back to the lab.

"This is the bull pen," she said, pushing open another set of double doors. "This is where all the cops, detectives, and everyone else resides."

I took in the rows of desks, each with a computer and cluttered with paper, half-empty coffee cups, and takeout containers. Offices flanked each side where I assumed the higher-ups on the force were located. Men and women walked around hurriedly. Some in uniform and others in street clothes. I blinked a few times, taking in the organized chaos until my eyes clashed on a giant of a man across the room with ice blue eyes staring straight at me.

I choked on a breath and fought to keep my eyes from widening. I would not let him know he had an effect on me. I lifted my chin and held his gaze until he was forced to look away when someone began talking to him. I still stared, hoping if I looked long enough it would be like contact therapy, and my heart would stop jumping up into my throat every time I'd see him.

He stood across the room, dressed casually in jeans and a long sleeve, gray Henley, that did nothing good for the pounding in my chest. I had to make sure my jaw was hinged closed from the way the shirt stretched across his broad shoulders.

"Girl, don't waste your time. As closed off as a wall, that one is." Laney interrupted my therapy session, dropping the same words that Evie and Luella used last night. "He's okay with the other detectives, and he's polite if not a little rough around the edges, but he isn't very friendly beyond that."

I let out a short laugh. "Oh, don't I know it," I said, recollecting his not so kind words from the other night. It had been a week and they still managed to knock the wind out of me. When Laney looked at me, eyebrows raised, I rushed to clarify. "He's my brother's best friend, but I don't see him much. They usually hangout around work-related things or go out for drinks."

"MacCabe," Laney said. "I thought your last name sounded familiar. Now Jack's nice. Especially when he brings some of Luella's cookies to share with everyone. Those delicious treats are always an added bonus when the station contracts his security company." She smiled before turning back toward the door. "Alright, I have a few more places to show you, then we can get back to the lab."

I followed Laney out but shot my eyes one last time back at Shane, who was looking at me again. I wished I was closer so I could see what those depths held, but all I'd probably see was that same blank stare.

Laney continued to point things out, but I was too consumed with the fact that Shane was here in this district building. What were the freaking chances? I wanted to tamp down the excitement and smother any hope. Stupid hope. Stupid imagination, hoping for anything positive to happen with him. Stupid memory trying to remind me of the look in his eyes when I'd dropped to my knees in front of him.

"We were lucky enough to get a small cafeteria added on recently," Laney said, bringing me back to the present. We walked into the last room on the tour, and my stomach grumbled at the smell of food wafting through the air. "It's not much, but better than a vending machine if you forget your lunch. Let's run back to the lab, grab our purses and we can come back and have something to eat. Then we can sit and you can ask me any questions you have up to this point."

I didn't really have any questions. Probably because my mind was consumed with thoughts of Shane for most of the tour, but I managed to think of a few while we ate. A couple of people from the lab sat with us at the bench-style seating and it was nice getting to know them.

When the doors opened again, I could tell it was Shane from the corner of my eye. He was taller than most and his broad shoulders were hard to miss. Plus, my body seemed to have developed a sixth sense where he was concerned, and zeroed in on his presence. Traitor.

He stared right at me, just as aware of my presence as I was of his, as he walked toward the lunch kiosk with a man next to him.

I tried to divert my eyes and focus on the others, laughing at the table, but it felt impossible. Even more so when the two men came over to our table.

"Hey, Laney." The man who walked in with Shane greeted Laney with a flirty smile.

She cocked her eyebrow in return, but responded. "Hey, Reese."

"This spot taken?" He asked gesturing to the open seats next to her. He didn't wait for an answer before sitting down. Shane sat beside him.

"Reese, this is Juliana." Laney introduced me. "She'll be training our new technicians on the lab equipment and procedures. Juliana, this is Reese Hill, the only man dumb enough to be partners with Shane over there."

Shane just grunted and stared down at his sandwich, but Reese stretched his arm across the table for me to shake. "Nice to meet you." His full lips stretched into a handsome smile.

Hmm. Shane's partner. It seemed like an interesting combination. Shane, with his lighter hair and eyes, and his closed-off personality. And then there was Reese, who was dark in contrast and seemed to have an easy smile for everyone. Maybe the two of them worked perfectly and used the good cop, bad cop routine.

"So, Juliana, do you have any plans this week?" Laney asked, returning to our conversation.

My eyes flicked to Shane who still wasn't looking at me. Coward. "Actually, I do. I've got a date on Friday." I made sure to say it loud enough so he couldn't even pretend not to hear.

"Oooh, good for you, girl. Where did you meet? Where is he taking you? Give me some details."

Again, I looked to Shane. This time he stared back at me from beneath his lashes. "I'm not sure where we're going. He's surprising me. But I met him at work. He works on the floor above me in the physics department."

Shane let out a loud scoff. "Sounds boring." Reese laughed and elbowed his partner.

I sent a withering glare in Shane's direction. He had no right to comment on my dates. What a dick.

"He sounds smart." Laney leaned past Reese and glared at Shane, before sitting back and waiting for more details. "What's he look like?"

"He's very sexy in that smart, nerdy kind of way. Very buff, but wears glasses. Think Clark Kent." I made myself sound more excited than I really felt. I wanted to make sure Shane knew I was fine without him. "And he's very smart. He's new at the university, just like me, so, we have that in common."

"I'm sure he's just as young and *cute* as you," Shane said, interrupting the excited oohs and ahs from Laney. "There's another thing you have in common with him. A little girl and a little boy on a sweet little date." One side of his mouth tipped up and leveled a challenging stare at me.

I wanted to slap him each time he said the word "little." And I didn't miss the way he reminded me of how "cute" he thought I was.

"Don't be mean to our new girl, Shane." Laney waved her hand in his direction. "Just because you have a cold heart doesn't mean we all have to be miserable."

"Burn." Reese laughed and Shane smacked the back of his head. Reese shook it off and turned to Laney with a smooth smile. "Hey, Laney, you know I have a heart of gold and would love to share it with you any time."

"Please." Laney chucked at Reese's come-on. "I know what you want to share with me and it isn't your *heart.* And what you do want to share with me . . ." Her eyes dropped to below his waist. "I'm gonna need more than that."

The table erupted in laughter and I thought I even saw Shane's lips twitch, but as soon as he caught me staring, they flattened again. Lunch moved quickly after that until we were all getting up to go back to work.

Before I could walk away, Shane gave me one last parting shot.

"Have fun on your *cute, little* date, Mini MacCabe."

Asshole.

Chapter Five

"There she is." My brother strode toward me from the bar as I entered an empty King's. Every Sunday everyone tried to meet up for brunch at Jameson's bar to catch up on each other's lives. It had started between Luella and her brother Jameson, then Evie started coming because I guess she was like a sister to Lu and is now dating Jameson, and then finally Jack came in once he started dating Lu. Because of Jack, I was invited to attend these weekly meet-ups. I didn't mind them, they were actually a lot of fun. They just weren't a priority.

The first month after I moved, I came religiously, my stupid heart pumping harder at the thoughts I'd conjured in my head with my stupid imagination. I would picture myself walking into the bar one day and finding Shane sitting there, waiting for me with a smile. He was part of the group, being so close to Jack, but behaved more like an outsider.

Of course, he never showed, and I was too much of a coward to ask if he ever came. Eventually, the brunches became less important and I spent my Sundays in my pajamas. Today though, Jo had a *friend* coming over and I promised I'd make myself scarce.

"I'm glad you decided to grace us with your presence this week," Jack said sarcastically.

Luella came up behind him and smacked his arm. "Ignore him."

"He's just lonely because he doesn't have another MacCabe to stick up for him." Evie chimed in from the table.

Luella rolled her eyes with a laugh. "Anyways. I hope you like pizza. We made enough for an army."

"I would never turn down pizza. Especially free pizza."

Before I could sit, Jack held me back by the door. "You have to call Mom and Dad more. They worry."

Translation? He was tired of getting phone calls asking for updates.

"I call them plenty. They don't need me to call every five seconds."

"Jules, you're the baby of the family. They worry."

"They let you go off to war and didn't give you shit when you moved here. So, what's the difference?"

"Because you were the unexpected surprise they always wanted. Mom and Dad would give you the world, but you know they're a little old fashioned about men's and women's roles."

I scoffed. "Oh yeah. I know. Like how they want me to stay close so they can take care of me until I find a strong suitable husband to step in. Maybe they can find a goat as a dowry."

"You're being dramatic."

"I'm not. I'm doing my best on my own, and it's frustrating when it feels like everyone around me is hoping I fail."

Jack's lips pinched. He tried to be neutral, but he always took on the big brother role. He was the only reason my parents hadn't had me kidnapped and taken back to Texas. They trusted him to keep an eye on me.

"We're not pushing you to fail. It's just hard for them to feel good about you so far away when you don't even keep in touch and drive a shitty car."

I dug my finger into his chest. "Betsy is wonderful and I won't have you talking about her like that."

"Betsy is a junker waiting to break down."

"She's mine and I paid for her. I earned her all on my own. Most parents would be proud of their child's independence."

"Most parents can't afford to buy both of their kids five cars each."

"Most parents wouldn't expect their daughter to stay home and be nothing more than a trophy wife." I took a deep breath to calm the anger rising up inside me. "Besides, I only need one car, and I choose Betsy."

He heaved a sigh and wrapped an arm around my shoulder. "Come on, let's drop it and go sit down."

"How's work going in the lab?" Lu asked once we all settled down.

"It's good. I had a pretty successful gel and we were able to collect some new data from that. Now it's just on to the western blot test." I explained my research knowing that she understood all the lingo since she worked in medical research. I ignored the way Evie rolled her eyes as we slipped into 'nerd-zone' as she called it.

"Oh, that's so exciting when something goes right. I swear it takes a thousand tries to move an inch," Lu said.

"We've talked about various ways of extracting the strand of DNA and putting it through individual tests. That is, if the professor leading the lab lets us."

"Why wouldn't he?"

"He's a misogynistic pig. He's one of those guys who looks down on women and questions everything we do. It takes ten times longer to do things because he wants us to report back to him on the most intermediate tasks."

"Ugh. What a douche."

The door to the bar opened, halting our conversation, and in walked the man I'd given up hope on ever showing up to a Sunday brunch. Too bad it was too late. I was no longer filled with excitement, but with disgust and frustration. Maybe anger. Too bad my body hadn't gotten the message. My pulse raced and my heart beat harder just seeing Shane's tall, broad frame fill the door.

"Oh, thank god!" Evie shouted, throwing her hands up in the air. "You saved us from our minds exploding listening to these two geek out. Thank you, Shane. You're my hero." She pressed her hands together under her chin and batted her eyelashes.

"Hey, now," Jameson said.

Evie laughed and leaned in to lay an uncomfortably long kiss on his lips.

"Ah, the elusive Shane *finally* shows. How many years have we been trying to get you to come?" Jack asked.

"Two, asshole. And I've showed up a few times." He took off his jacket and walked toward the table, doing his best to not look at me, but I caught his eyes flick in my direction at least twice before he finally sat. Right across from me. My lips twitched at how miserable he probably was at the seating arrangement.

"Shane, you remember Juliana." Jack introduced me, thinking we'd only seen each other twice.

"Vaguely," Shane said.

Asshole. Such an asshole. "You're so full of shit," I said, rolling my eyes. "I saw Shane earlier this week and will continue to see him about twice a week now that I have that position at the station."

I'd told Jack about the work I'd be doing in the forensic lab when I'd first learned about it. He was happy for me, but it was Luella who sat me down after dinner and asked me all kinds of questions. God, I loved having a sister who understood my love of science.

"Oh, hey, I didn't realize that you'd be at Shane's station," Jack said.

Shane nodded his thanks to Jameson for the beer he brought him, and muttered, "Neither did I," before taking a long pull.

"Sounds like you're both *thrilled* to be so close to each other." Evie laughed at her own sarcastic comment.

"Well, this is great," Jack said. "Shane make sure you take care of her. I know how those assholes can be at the station. Bunch of perverts."

"Speaking of perverts." Evie clapped her hands and gave me a wink. "How is dating all the men in Cincinnati going?"

"I don't want to hear about my sister's love life," Jack whined.

"Hush. Let the girl talk," Evie said. "It's Sunday brunch. Everyone shares."

Jack leveled a stare at Jameson, probably some guy code to control your woman, but Jameson just wrapped an arm around Evie and drank from his beer. Evie was not one to be controlled.

"Meh. It's okay." I shrugged and reached for my glass of wine, spinning it on the table. "I had a date Friday, but it just wasn't going well." I took a drink and looked across the table at Shane to find him smirking at me. "But after he left, I stayed for another drink and ended up meeting someone. We have a date tonight." I held his icy gaze the whole time, his smirk falling to a flat line.

Luella catcalled and Evie said, "You go girl."

"Jules, do you think it's smart to be dating so much?"

I turned to my brother and gave him a blank stare. "I'm going to pretend you didn't just say that. Or I'll have to start bringing up your earlier years, and I'd hate to do that in front of your wife."

He stared at me, irritated, and drank from his beer rather than respond. But when Shane let a choked laugh slip out, Jack leveled his glare on him. "Don't even get me started on you, manwhore."

Luella spoke up—loudly. "Anyhoo . . . Anyone else have anything fascinating to share?"

Evie had a new overseas fashion project that could make her a bigger designer than she already was. Jameson was set to open his new bar next month, expanding King's to a new area. Jack regaled us with stories about the types of clients that came in and tried to hire his security services. And Luella and I lost our-selves in conversation when she started talking about her project at work.

"So, what about you Shane? Anything new in your life?" Lu asked.

"Any new ladies?" Evie taunted.

Jealousy set fire to my blood. He may not have wanted me, but I didn't want to sit there and listen to him talk about women he thought were more worthy than me. I stared at him, waiting for his answer. He leaned back in his chair, his long legs stretched out in front of him, ankles crossed as one hand casually turned his beer. He looked like he didn't have a care in the world, while I sat there, each second tightening my muscles a little more.

Finally, he put me out of my misery.

"Not really. No one to bring home to mom."

Jack laughed. "You don't have a mom."

They both laughed like it was an inside joke, but my chest pinched at the possible reasons why he didn't have a mom. Had she died? Were they estranged? I had to bite my tongue to keep from asking.

"Even if I did have one."

"Well, maybe we can keep you roped into coming to these get-togethers, and one day you'll walk through the door with some lucky lady on your arm."

I swallowed hard when Shane leveled me with a stare across the table. He lifted his beer for a drink and before it touched his lips, he muttered, "Maybe."

That one word seemed to have more weight than what it seemed. At least, it weighed on me. I thought about it the rest of brunch and on my drive home, completely distracted. The idea of him walking into the bar with his hand wrapped in someone else's taunted me.

It wasn't until I was getting out of my car that I checked my phone and saw a text from Hudson that made me want to throw my phone.

Hudson: You know I still love you right. If you're worried about being alone here, I just want to reassure you that you were always the one for me. Call me later.

Still loved me? It had been so long and I'd already changed so much. What would he think of me if I told him about my night with Shane, about the things I now craved from a man? Things Hudson had never given me. Would he be so eager to have me then?

Chapter Six

I jogged down the hall to our lab at school. Today was a day I was supposed to be at the department, but first I needed to grab an updated book on some of the equipment. The technicians were quick to pick up the protocols and this book was a great tool. I turned the corner and bumped into a wall. Well, maybe not exactly a wall, I realized as I stumbled back and stared up into a pair of smiling brown eyes.

"Whoa. Careful there." Dr. Voet gripped my upper arms to help keep me on my feet. "Where's the fire?"

I laughed. "No fire, just trying to run in for a book." I swallowed, always nervous around him, and brushed my hair back from my face. "Sorry about that."

"No worries." His grip loosened and his hands dragged down to my elbows before letting go. That was normal. A harmless, normal gesture. "I'm glad I ran into you—or actually you into me. I wanted to ask you how things were going at the police department."

"Great. They have all new equipment and, not that I would admit to anyone, I may have Googled how to turn on the HPLC. Turns out they moved the on switch to the other side."

"It's always the smallest things that trip us up. And how are the technicians? Are they picking up on it okay?"

"Yeah, they're doing great. Really fast learners and they ask all the right questions. Thank goodness."

"Good. One of them used to do research in my lab a few years ago. Frank, I think."

"Oh, yeah. Frank is really funny and very smart." Frank was probably too advanced to be a technician, but said he didn't have the time to devote to going to grad school.

"Well, I won't keep you. I just wanted to check in to see how it was going, and I always seem to miss you on the days you're here. Keep up the good work." I almost choked on my tongue when his hand patted my shoulder and then dragged down my arm before he walked away. I tried to decide if the giggle bubbling up my throat was from nerves or excitement at the overly familiar touch.

"Lingering in the hallway is unacceptable and a waste of time," Jolene said in a deep voice behind me. I turned and rolled my eyes. "Don't let Dr. Stahl see you. You know how much he hates when you waste time instead of slaving away over his notes."

I walked alongside her to our room. "I'm just swinging by to grab a book and then I'm heading out."

"Well, you can take five minutes to give me the DL. I feel like we're ships passing in the night and never have time to catch up at work."

"Not my fault you have a man to keep you busy."

She bit her lip and smiled. "I know, I know. But he makes my late nights at his place worth it."

I smirked. "I bet he does."

"Okay. Tell me. How is the station with Shane, and how was your date Sunday night?"

"Honestly, other than that one time, I haven't really seen Shane at the station. They keep me locked away with all the pretty new equipment."

"Ugh, bitch. I'm so jealous of all your cool toys."

"Don't be too jealous. My date Sunday was a bust. He was a total creeper. I think he applied four thousand coats of Chapstick throughout the night. And would only drink half a cup of water before demanding a fresh, new one. Also, his hand tapped against the table the entire meal. So annoying."

"Wow. Sounds . . .Awesome. Were his lips at least soft at the end of the night?" she asked, sounding hopeful.

"Er. I wouldn't know because I was not going to even try."

"Are you giving up? I know this weekend was a bust."

"Hell, no. I met another guy at the supermarket on Tuesday, and he's taking me out Saturday."

"Yes, girl." She lifted her hand for a high-five.

"Okay, I have to get going. Let's make a date for ice cream, pizza, and movies soon."

"You had me at ice cream."

Mercifully, I made it out of the building without running into Dr. Stahl. Last time I saw him, he gave me a disapproving speech about falling behind in my research, and informed me that he knew it was hard for a woman to multitask effectively, but to at least try. I thought I was going to need to make an appointment with the dentist after grinding my teeth through that talk. He was such a dick.

When I strolled into the lab, Laney greeted me with a smile. "Before you get settled can you take this up to the Chief? They're the results he's waiting on for a case."

"Sure." I set my purse down and hung up my coat before heading to the bullpen. Was Shane working? Would he stare at me as I walked past his desk toward the Chief's office? I wore a new pair of slacks, and they made my ass look fantastic if I had to say myself. Would he imagine gripping each cheek and hoisting me against the wall and grind into my core? Maybe he'd follow me out and corner me in a supply closet, unable to control himself.

Stop! I squeezed my eyes shut, forcing my imagination to quit with the possibilities. He probably wasn't there, just like he hadn't been there the entire week.

Except that he was there, and as soon as I saw his dirty blond hair across the room, I stood a little taller, swayed my hips a little harder in case he looked. And he did look. I'd made it about halfway to the office when his eyes zeroed in on me. I smiled—to be polite—not because my heart skipped a beat in my chest and butterflies fluttered in my stomach. My body would never be so traitorous.

Unfortunately, his eyes didn't track to my ass looking fantastic. Instead, he gave me his signature blank stare.

I softly knocked on the open door.

"Come in," a gruff voice responded.

I walked in and smiled awkwardly at the large man with dark mocha skin behind the desk. "Mr. Pearson."

"Yes?"

I stepped forward and held out the file. "I'm Juliana. From the forensic lab. Laney asked me to bring these up to you." As soon as I explained who I was his expression went from irritated to relaxed and smiling.

"Ah, yeah, Ms. MacCabe. I've heard a lot about you from Jack. I should've recognized you since you both have the same blue eyes."

"I get that a lot."

He stood and took the file, but blindly set it on his desk, still smiling at me. "How are you liking the Queen City?"

"I love it. Cincinnati is beautiful."

"Good. Good. Well if you ever need anything, you let me know, and we'll be sure to help however we can. We like to take care of our own here."

"Thank you, Sir."

I walked out the door and only managed to take two steps before I ran into another wall. "Dammit." I swore at my clumsiness and stumbled back, looking up into a pair of familiar light eyes.

"How was your date, Mini MacCabe?"

I didn't know why he was asking. By his condescending tone, probably just to taunt me, but I wasn't going to give him the opportunity. I plastered a big smile on my face. "It was fantastic. He was a real gentleman. Hot. Such a strong *man*."

I accentuated the word 'man' as a rebuttal to all the times he told me I should go date little boys.

He laughed under his breath and stepped closer. "Did he take you home? Kiss you goodnight?" he asked, his voice deep and gruff.

I swallowed past the dryness in my throat. He was closer to me than he'd been since our night in Jamaica, which wasn't saying much, but it still kicked up my heart rate. "A lady never kisses and tells, Shane."

Another step, this time almost coming into contact with me. I struggled to keep my aloof composure when he went one step further and leaned closer to my face.

He hummed. "Did he find out what you sound like when you scream? Moan? Come? Does he know that you taste rich and decadent?"

My eyes dropped to his lips as they formed the words. My mind scrambled to form a response. Taking in his words, I replayed the way he made me scream, moan, and come as he figured out how I tasted.

"Shane." I breathed his name, unable to control the small pants puffing past my lips. "Why do you care?" I didn't understand why he would push me away, make fun of my dates, and then taunt me with what had happened between us. He had to know what his words were doing to me. I just didn't understand why he was saying them.

He opened his mouth and took an incremental step forward.

One more inch and we'd be chest to chest.

"I didn't do it!" A shout came from the front of the office. "I swear. Get your hands off me." Our heads jerked in the direction of the commotion and saw two officers bringing in a man who clearly seemed to be resisting.

I took in the dirty jeans and white t-shirt, looking up to find a familiar face. "Oh, shit."

There, being dragged into the station, was my date. The one I'd just been talking up.

"What?" Shane asked beside me.

I stepped back and tried to turn my body, but the motion drew the man's attention.

"Hey! Hey, baby," he directed at me. Then turned to the two cops over his shoulder. "She can tell you. Her. Baby, tell them I would never be a creeper. I'm a good guy." The whole station turned to look at me—Baby. "She knows. We went on a date. Tell them Julie. Baby! Julie!"

My face flamed. I dropped my head and worked to take subtle, deep breaths to help control the way my blood was pounding underneath my skin. I could feel Shane's eyes on me, and I seriously considered just running out without looking at him. Maybe I'd never have to see him again.

"It wasn't me," he said again. "That lady was lying about me jerking it to her. And even so, maybe she shouldn't leave her blinds open. She was wanting me to see her." I cringed and felt a little sick that I sat across from him for an hour over dinner. "Julie!" he shouted one last time as they took him through the door.

Shane chuckled next to me, and I glared at him from beneath my lashes, still not facing him head on.

"Sounds like a good date, *Julie*. Can't wait to see who you date next."

"Fuck you." It was a real mature response. And his laughter as I stormed away was really the icing on the cake.

Chapter Seven

I rotated my body so I could only see my left side in the mirror and then turned again to look at my right, comparing which shoe I should wear on my date. The black pump or the over the knee suede boots. Maybe I should've scrapped both options and gone for flats. Being five-foot-ten made wearing heels on a date a risk. Some guys got intimidated by my height.

But I felt confident with heels, so if the guy was that easy to scare off, then fuck him. I settled on the boots. I liked the way they matched my sweater. Sitting on my bed, I pulled the other boot on when I heard my phone vibrate on the nightstand. I picked it up and opened the message, immediately regretting it.

Mom: Hey sweetie. Just checking in. How are you?

Mom: We miss you.

Mom: I was talking to a lady at the country club today and she said there was a volunteer position opening up at the hospital near home. That way you could still work in your science-y stuff and be close to us.

Mom: Hudson came by today. I think he really misses you.

My science-y stuff? I took deep breaths trying to calm my frustration. My mom didn't fully understand what my degree was in, but it had nothing to do with volunteering at a hospital. Not that there was anything wrong with it, but when you slave over a degree for as long as I had, you wanted to use it to its full potential. It was a slap in the face for her to assume I'd give up what I had here just to go home.

And as though he knew my mom had just mentioned him, a text from Hudson came through.

Hudson: Your mom told me she offered you money for a better car and you turned it down. We get it Juliana, you're an independent adult. But you don't have to be dumb about it.

My face heated as I stared at his message. Dumb? *Dumb?* I had to toss the phone aside to prevent myself from sending back a scathing response. Hudson had hidden his hope for me to be his trophy wife better than my parents had, but it was still obvious he hoped I'd fall in line like the other women we'd grown up with. What he so conveniently ignored, was that money from my parents came with a string that tugged me away from the life I was building here.

I stomped across the hall to the bathroom like a petulant child and put the final touches on my makeup. After my last dating fiasco, I said I wouldn't do it again, but I was at a coffee shop when he approached me. He'd been so freaking handsome, my heart had skipped in excitement. He'd sat across from me and been so humble and kind that when he asked if we could meet for drinks tonight, I couldn't say no. I didn't want to.

I put the mascara away and stared at my reflection. Maybe it would work out, and I could bring him to the next family brunch, maybe even make Shane jealous. My plum-colored lips tipped up at the idea. He would be so jealous that he'd missed out. He'd rage when he saw my hand in my new boyfriend's. He'd corner me in the back hall and tell me what a mistake he'd made and set about convincing me with his hands and mouth.

Wait.

No.

Not that.

Shaking my head, I collected my phone and ordered an Uber. We were meeting at a bar in Over the Rhine, and I didn't want to worry about driving. Also, I wanted to impress him. As much as I loved Betsy, she wasn't for everyone.

The Uber dropped me off at Sundry and Vice. I saw him leaning against the outside wall, his dark head bent over his phone.

"Jacob." I called his name and he lifted his head before walking toward me. The looked he gave me warmed my core.

"Juliana. Wow." Once he was closer, my heels brought us eye to eye and I was pleased to see that he didn't seem to mind. He took my arm and led me into the crowded bar. It was small and reminded me of an old London pub, with a bar along the wall on one side and about five booths along the windows on the other side. Thankfully, we found one of the booths open and grabbed a seat.

"You look beautiful." His green eyes twinkled at me and I giggled like a school girl.

This was it. This was going to be the date I'd been waiting for. Butterflies took flight in my stomach and we ordered our first drink. Jacob asked for top shelf bourbon in his Old Fashioned and it made me like him even more. He had such confidence and an inclination for the nicer things in life. I followed suit and didn't hesitate when I ordered my drink, despite the price.

We fell into easy conversation about our lives. He worked in marketing and had always lived in Cincinnati. I told him about my job in research, and he seemed as if he was really trying to understand what I was explaining.

Thankfully, we got that out of the way earlier in the night, because as the night went on, his drink orders started coming faster and I struggled to keep up. When my face started to feel numb I asked for a water.

"Tell me about your family. You said you aren't from around here, so where did you come from?" His deep voice washed over my tingling body and encouraged me to share.

And share I did. I told him about my family wanting me to come back home. I shared how they wanted to pay for my whole life as long as I remained the perfect Southern belle. I explained how I wanted to be an independent woman.

"Oh, so you're rich," Jacob said.

"Ummm," I hesitated over my words because where I came from, money wasn't really something we talked about specifically. "I guess my family is. But, like I said, I won't take their money."

"But you could. So technically, you're just as well off."

"I guess." I shrugged off the statement, turning the conversation, asking about Cincinnati.

He began slurring through his words, but so did I. We were having fun. Laughing. Our hands touched in the middle of the table and it sent goose bumps up my arm. Maybe I'd take him home with me.

"Hey, I'm going to go to the bathroom. Be right back."

"Okay."

As soon as he walked through the door, I pulled out a compact and touched up my lipstick. I wanted to look my best when he came back. I was going to ask him to leave with me. It was just before twelve-thirty according to my phone and the night was coming to a close.

I waited, watching the door.

Then I waited some more.

I brought my phone to life and checked the time. Twelve-forty-two.

I was just about to get up and go check on him when a waitress stopped by me, sliding a piece of paper across the table. "The man in the back asked me to give this to you."

She gave me a polite smile and walked away.

I opened the note and my heart sank to the floor.

Thanks babe! Had to go. I'm sure you can afford it anyways.
XOXO

Son of a bitch. Hot tears burned the backs of my eyes, and I closed my fist around the piece of paper. I downed the rest of my drink and gathered myself. Deep breaths. I thought about running out after him and making him come back and pay. Groaning inwardly, I tried to calculate how bad this was going to be. Probably the equivalent to my half of the rent. Shit. I was going to have to dip into my savings.

Why did I order such fancy drinks? Why did I just assume he would've paid? At least my drinks weren't as expensive as his, even if he did have twice as many as me. I snatched my purse off the seat and approached the bar, wiggling between the crowd in front of the register.

"Can I help you?" a bartender with a handlebar mustache asked.

"Yeah. Can I have the check for the table over there?" I pointed at the booth I'd vacated.

He cocked an eyebrow at me and asked, "All of it?"

"Yup. My date ditched me and left me with the bill."

He pulled up the check and printed it off, slipping it inside an old book and sliding it over to me.

Slowly, I opened the pages, peaking inside like it was a snake about to bite me. Three-hundred and seventy-six dollars. I almost threw up the last drink I'd had. Fuck, this was painful.

"Looks like you found a winner, Mini MacCabe," an all too familiar voice said next to me.

Nope. The bill was no longer the most painful thing. Having Shane there to witness my complete and utter humiliation was soul crushing. I looked to my right at the man who haunted both my dreams and my nightmares.

He met my glare with a smile before bringing a tumbler of amber liquid to his lips.

I growled and jabbed my hand into my purse, searching for my wallet. Before I could get my card out, a large hand with strong fingers held out a silver card to the bartender.

"I've got this, Andre."

"No, Shane." I didn't need his help. I could face my mistakes without being saved. "I won't take your money. I can pay for it myself." I held my chin high, showing no weakness.

"I know you can. But you're not. Consider it the city paying for the dick-holes on the street," he said to me before addressing Andre. "Add another drink for her too."

"What?" I turned my whole body to face him rather than just staring at him from the corner of my eyes. He looked delicious. Gray buttoned up shirt with the sleeves rolled up past his thick forearms. A tie hanging loosely around the collar. And a leather jacket draped across the back of his chair. "No, Shane."

He completely ignored my demand as the bartender finished the transaction and handed him back his card. "Sit, Mini Mac-Cabe. Relax."

I begrudgingly sat and pulled my fresh drink close to me. "Seriously," I muttered miserably. "You just had to be here. Shouldn't you be in a hole by yourself?"

"Shouldn't you be on a date?" Placing his elbow on the bar, he leaned his head on his fist and smirked at me. "You sure know how to pick 'em."

I took a drink avoiding his eyes, forming my defense. "I'm testing the waters. Being free of my parents and my ex and their expectations." I copied his position and stared into his icy eyes, letting him know he didn't scare me. "If I want to date them all, then I will."

"Seems to be going great so far." He smiled. "Can't wait to see how it goes from here on out."

The asshole was laughing at me.

"Oh, and you can do sooo much better. You have some wise wisdom to impart, Yoda?"

"Of course, I do. I'm much older than you. More experience and more wisdom." The way he growled, it made me imagine he was frustrated with our age difference.

"Fine," I said with a challenging smile.

I snatched his phone from where it was on the counter and pulled up the text messages. Surprisingly, he didn't grab it back or say anything, instead just cocked an eyebrow. I entered my contact info and sent a message to myself.

"I'll be sure to let you know how the next date goes and get your wisdom on the experience about what I can do better."

"Juliana," he said, a warning note in his voice.

"We're friends now. You're welcome." I downed the rest of my drink and hopped off the stool. "Night, Shane." With a finger wave, I held his eyes until I exited through the door, hoping that behind his frustration with me, there was the pulse of excitement too.

Chapter Eight

I couldn't *believe* I had forgotten to pay the electric bill. Way to show everyone what a mature adult you are, Juliana.

I ignored the taunting voice in my head and hopped on one foot toward the door as I put my boot on the other.

Thankfully, no one was there to witness my idiocy. Jolene had gone home over the weekend to visit family, and apparently, also meeting future husband possibilities. She sounded super stoked when we talked. I told her to ask them if they were into platonic sister-wives so we wouldn't ever have to separate. That at least got a smile out of her.

I scrambled to find my phone, keys, and the bill. Technically, it wasn't late yet. If I could make it to the building by noon, then I wouldn't owe a late fee. But there was no chance of mailing it in with it due tomorrow, on a Sunday. Cue eye roll.

I'd never been late on a bill before, but I'd been so caught up with extra research material Dr. Stahl had given me. Because he hated me. Hell, he hated everyone, but for someone who was striving for success on her own, he was making it more difficult for me. It didn't matter that I had strict orders to be at the forensic lab twice a week, he'd scoffed and stared down his nose at me.

"Since you're off gallivanting around, Jolene has had to take on more TA work with the useless undergrad student," he had snarled at me. "She has fallen behind on research, so I expect you to pick up the slack. Have these read by Monday with a plan ready for the week."

He'd tossed a stack of research articles that would take anyone a month to read through. So, my mind had been a little frantic over the week, trying to cram as much information in as possible. If I hadn't taken a small break to eat, then I would've completely forgotten the bill that sat on the kitchen counter under my Chinese take-out menu.

Now I was about to be a frantic failure without power if I didn't haul ass. Dramatic? Yep.

Slipping my last boot on, my phone began to vibrate in my hand. I almost drop it on the tile when at the last minute I caught it, bringing it to my ear with a breathless, "Hello?"

"Hey, Jules." Hudson's voice boomed through the phone.

"Hey, Hudson." I locked the door and jogged down my apartment stairs toward Betsy.

"I was calling to check in. I haven't heard your voice in a while. I miss you."

"Oh, yeah. I've been busy with work and everything." I purposefully ignored the 'I miss you' comment. "How are you?"

"Yeah, yeah. I'm good. Got a promotion at work last week."

"That's great, Hudson. I know you love working for my dad." I put my key into the ignition and said a silent prayer that Betsy would turn over on the first try. I didn't need Hudson to hear her struggle and start in on me again.

"I do. Your parents had me and my family over for dinner this week." I struggled to follow the quick topic change from work to my parents. "They asked me if I'd mention to you maybe calling more."

"Hudson," I said, hoping he'd catch the warning note in my voice.

"They miss you, Jules. We all do."

"I know. But that's just the way it is. My life is here now."

Hudson and I had been friends since we were in diapers. We got in trouble together, played together, did everything together. We were each other's first everything, too. It was no secret that our families expected us to end up together. And with me leaving, it had changed the future they had imagined for me.

They had been upset when Hudson and I broke up, but I guessed they'd expected me to go to grad school and come back to my rightful place by his side. I threw a curve ball to their plans when I left. I hadn't realized Hudson had been expecting me to return to his side too until he'd dropped that huge bomb on me at the airport. But it was too late. I had never felt passion with Hudson. It was more like comfort. That comfort had become even more apparent after my night with Shane, which lit me on fire in ways I'd never experienced. I just couldn't go back to Hudson after that.

"What happened to us Jules? Weren't we happy together?"

This wasn't the conversation I wanted to have as I sped through the streets trying to get my bill dropped off on time.

"Of course we were. Just . . .Maybe not in the way we should have been."

"What do you mean? Did I not satisfy you? Because the way I remember it, I satisfied you many times."

I laughed uncomfortably, not wanting to talk about our past sex life. "Did you honestly feel a fiery passion with me? If you did, then why did you let me walk away so easily?"

"Because it's what I thought you needed, and time away would make you realize how great we were."

"No, Hudson. I walked away because I wanted to feel more."

"I refuse to believe we're completely over. If you need to get it out of your system, then fine. But I'll be here, waiting for you."

"I'm sorry, Hudson. I have to go." I hung up before he could respond. I didn't know what to say anyway.

Finally, I pulled up to the building at twelve-ten. Traffic had been a bitch, but maybe someone was still there and would let me in. I parked and walked up to the door and of course no one was there. The place sat dark and barren. A sign on the door read that all weekend payments could be dropped off at the slot on the side of the building.

At least I wouldn't be late.

I walked around and slipped my payment in, feeling satisfaction at having it done, just as the skies opened and buckets of rain poured down on me. I pulled my jacket tight and ran toward Betsy, getting soaked on the way. Freaking end of February was just cold enough to chill me to my bones, but not cold enough for snow.

I got in and blasted my heat, which decided to take forever to get going, but at that point, I was okay with even slightly warm air.

"Come on, Betsy," I said, stroking the dash. "We just got to make it home. Mama will take you to the spa and get you an oil change and checkup. Just warm me up, baby."

However, a couple blocks later, Betsy gave up on me. She sadly puttered, and I had enough sense to coast over to the shoulder. I placed her in park and tried to get the ignition to turn over. A couple of false starts, and then nothing. The lights came on, but the engine was dead.

"Betsy. Baby. Don't do this. I've defended you to everyone. Don't let me down, girl."

I closed my eyes and whispered a quick prayer before turning the key.

Nothing.

"God dammit!" I yelled. "No! No, no, no!" Every word was punctuated by me smacking the steering wheel. Frustrated tears burned the backs of my eyes and I clenched my jaw to hold them back, but it was useless. The day, the week, the conversation with Hudson, it all caught up with me. I let my forehead fall to the leather of the steering wheel and cried. Who was I going to call? The obvious choice would be Jack. He'd know what to do. But my pride refused to give in.

He'd look at me with this I-told-you-so look. Then he'd call my mom and dad and I'd be fucked. And I couldn't call anyone else because they'd all talk about it at Sunday brunch, and I'd sit there like a shamed child.

After letting a few more tears fall, I sat up and wiped my cheeks, taking a deep breath and tried to think until a light bulb went off.

Shane.

He was a cop, he had to help me. And he didn't really chit chat with anyone, so it'd be fine. I'd just have to ask him to not tell Jack. A part of me didn't want him to see me like this, but he'd already seen me low, so whatever. He was the lesser of two evils.

I pulled out my phone and scrolled until I found his name. It rang once before he picked up.

"Have a date so soon after the last awesome adventure?" His tone teased me, but it was all I needed to hear, and dammit, if I didn't embarrass myself even further when I started to cry.

"Sh-Shane."

"What's wrong? Where are you?"

Immediately his tone changed to serious, falling into cop mode.

"I'm fine. So-sorry. My car broke down and I didn't want to call Jack because he would just get on my case and I can't, I can't have any more today. I didn't know who else to call." It all poured out of me and I could hear his sigh through the phone.

"Okay. Have you called insurance for a tow?"

"Umm, no. I didn't know I needed to." I was such a novice and felt like an idiot admitting everything I didn't know.

"Where are you?" I gave him my location. "Stay in your car with the doors locked. I'll be there shortly."

As soon as I hung up, I dropped my phone into the passenger seat and pulled down my visor to check myself in the mirror and wipe away any stray mascara trailing down my cheeks. I did the best I could with a paper napkin I found in the glovebox, and then closing my eyes, I took some deep, steadying breaths to try and calm down. Shane had heard me lose my cool; he didn't need to see what a hot mess I looked like on top of it.

Once I looked a little less horrifying, I began searching for my insurance card. I was pulling it out, as Shane nosed his car in behind me.

He came around to the passenger side and I unlocked the door to let him in. The rain had slowed, but not stopped. Water dripped down his temples and the bridge of his nose.

"I found my insurance card." I held up the piece of paper like it was the answer to all our problems. He was nice enough not to laugh at me.

"Good. Why don't you go ahead and call them? Let them know you broke down and need a tow. But first, try and turn the engine over for me. Let me hear it."

I pushed me keys into the ignition and hoped that Betsy would both start, so I could avoid whatever was wrong with her, and also not start because I would feel like the biggest tool bag for making a mess out of nothing.

Taking a deep breath, I turned the key. Silence. The lights came on, but the ignition didn't do a damn thing.

"Well, it's not your battery. Besides that, it could be about anything."

"That narrows it down."

He ignored my sarcastic comment. "Pop the hood and let me see if I notice anything off."

"Okay." I started looking along my dash around my wheel for something that looked like it popped my hood. Apparently, I took too long, because Shane's long arm reached across my chest and pulled a lever by my steering wheel. My breathing stuttered at having him so close, his body slightly leaned over mine, the heat from his skin reaching across the small space between us to light me on fire. He was so close, I had to fight from leaning forward to bury my lips against his neck and licking the drop of water that slowly slid down his sharp jaw.

A blush worked its way up into my cheeks from my thoughts, but deepened when he gave me a slightly exasperated look, making my embarrassment at looking so dumb impossible to hide. Miss I-want-to-be-independent couldn't even pop her own damn hood.

Thankfully, if he noticed, he didn't acknowledge it before getting out and moving around the front of my car. While he peeked under the hood, I called my insurance company and stumbled through answering all the questions. By the end of the conversation, I had been taken down a peg on how smart I thought I was. I had a Master's in biochemistry and could break down the parts of a cell, but I could barely make an insurance claim. So much for college.

Shane climbed back in a couple of minutes after I ended the call. He was drenched. His light hair looked almost brown as it clung to his forehead. I clenched my fists to stop myself from dragging my fingers across his forehead and pushing it back to stop the water dripping down his face.

"I don't see anything obvious out of the ordinary, so it's going to have to be taken to a shop. They may get a chance to look at it today, but if not, they probably won't until Monday."

"Dammit. I guess I'll have to see if Jolene can give me a ride. Or I'll have to ride the bus."

"Don't ride the bus."

"I don't have much choice."

"You have lots of choices. Jack—"

"I am *not* asking Jack for help. He barely thinks I'm capable as it stands. If he found out about this, he'd jump ship to Mom and Dad's side and probably cart me back to Texas himself."

"Okay." Shane dragged the words out and lifted his hands in defeat. "Just, don't ride the bus. They're not always the safest places. Call me if you need a ride and, if I can't give you one, I'll find someone who can."

"Thank you," I muttered, my eyes glued to my lap. "The tow should be here soon."

"Good. We'll get you all squared away and then I'll get you home."

"Thank you," I said again.

We didn't wait long before the truck arrived. We were going to follow him to the shop, but the driver told me there was no point. They wouldn't be able to work on it today. He said they'd call me with an update, then he looked me over, shivering and wet in the cold rain, and told me to hurry home before I got sick.

Shane escorted me to his car and blasted the heat. Actual heat. Not the pitiful gasps of warm air Betsy struggled to give off.

"Listen," Shane said with his hands gripping the steering wheel, the car still in park. "I live right around the corner. Let me take you there and get you warmed up. I've got some soup too, and then I'll take you home."

"I can take care of myself." I sounded like an ungrateful snotty child, as I sat shivering in the seat.

"I know. Just . . .Just let me get you warm."

Biting my lip, I watched his profile and my imagination took off. How would he keep me warm? Why did he care so much? He probably missed me and was using this opportunity to get close to me. The idea warmed me more than the heat coming through the air vents.

However, the snug image I had created in my head shattered with his next words.

"If Jack ever does find out about this, at least I can say I took care of his little sister and maybe he'd spare me some mercy."

Chapter Nine

Shane's garage had about ten spots for the residents in the converted corner building. Cincinnati had converted a lot of its older factories into condos and apartments. They were all gorgeous and Shane's place was a lot more put together than I'd expected for a bachelor.

"I'm not a heathen, Juliana," he said, watching me stare around his modern apartment in awe.

"I know. I just didn't expect it to be so decorated, I guess."

"If you want to call hanging curtains decoration, then sure."

But it wasn't just the curtains. It was the way they draped on the floor with elegance. It was the black and white photos of Cincinnati hanging on the exposed brick wall mixed with a few personal photos. It was the throw blanket that matched the pillows on the sectional couch. In my mind, Shane had been a playboy bachelor with pizza boxes, beers, and condoms littering his loft apartment. This image didn't mesh with the one I was seeing now.

"Well, it's a nice place."

"Thank you." His response was short and gruff and it made me think that maybe he was embarrassed by someone seeing that side of him. "Let me get changed and I'll bring you some warm clothes to change in to."

He disappeared down a short hall. I imagined him stripping off his wet clothes and the rivulets of water trailing down each ridge of his abs. But then I didn't have to imagine because I remembered the way he'd looked standing naked in the shower in Jamaica when he'd told me to turn around and brace my hands on the wall.

I jumped when he rounded the corner and tossed some clothes at me. I muttered a quick thanks, keeping my head down so he couldn't see the flush staining my cheeks as I walked past him.

"You'll probably have to hold them up, but they're the smallest pair I have."

"Thanks."

Then I stood in his room and it looked more like a man's space. The bed was unmade with dark gray sheets and comforter. One nightstand with a lamp and glasses, and a dresser completed the room. There was only one picture on the wall of the precinct. The rest of the walls were blank. It felt intimate standing in the middle of his bedroom as I stripped off my wet clothes. I thought about keeping my bra and underwear on, but they were soaked. Besides, my small breasts wouldn't be noticeable under the baggy T-shirt he'd given me.

Balling everything up, I walked over to where he stood in the kitchen, pulling containers out of the fridge.

"You can toss those in the dryer just around the corner."

I walked past the open kitchen, finding the stackable appliances and threw my clothes in, hoping they took forever to dry, giving me more time with him.

When I returned he was pouring what looked to be soup out of the containers into a pot on the stove.

"You didn't have to go through this much trouble," I said, sitting on a stool at the island, watching his back muscles ripple with every move under his black T-shirt.

"It's not much. I had leftover chicken noodle. Hope you don't mind."

"It sounds great. Thank you."

"Do the clothes fit?" he asked, glancing over his shoulder at me.

"I had to roll the boxers up and they're still a little loose. Just don't let me go bouncing around anywhere, and I won't be in any danger of them falling off."

A grunt was all I got in return for my joke. Okay, then. I watched him grab bowls and ladle soup into each before bringing both steaming bowls over to me.

"Beer? Water?"

"A beer would be great."

He sat our drinks down and then sat on the stool beside me, not saying anything as he ate. I took his cue and remained silent until we'd finished. And as awkward as it sounded, it was actually really comfortable. He sat so close that his body heat was warming me up faster than the soup. I fought to not lean into him and let my arm graze his. I fought to not turn on the stool and let my foot glide up his sweatpants and feel his strong leg flex under my touch.

He finished before me and took long pulls from his beer. I struggled to keep from smiling when I felt his gaze on me. It wasn't direct, but enough that it stoked the fire simmering beneath my skin.

Setting my spoon down, I grabbed my beer and turned to face him, holding his eyes as I brought the bottle to my mouth. His gaze dropped to my lips when I licked the residual beer from them.

"So, why don't you come to the Sunday brunches?" I decided to break the silence before I climbed on his lap and begged him to lick my lips for me. Begged him to lick all of me. Begged him to let me lick all of him.

"It's a family thing, and other than being close to Jack, I'm not family. I'm out of place there."

"Well, other than Jack it's not really my family either. But that's the point. It's more of a hodge-podge, create-your-own-family."

"I guess I'm not very family-oriented."

"What do you do with your family?" I asked hesitantly, remembering his comment about not having a mother.

"Don't have one." He turned away and pulled from his beer once he answered. I got the idea that maybe I was treading into a touchy subject, but having this man in front of me—finally—encouraged me to push for more. I wanted to know him, even if he wanted to ignore me.

"What happened to them?"

His teeth dragged across his lip as he scratched at the label on his beer. "Never knew my dad, and my mom died of a drug overdose. So, I was put in foster care."

"Shane. I'm so sorry," I whispered, my hand reaching out to touch his shoulder.

He turned his blue eyes to me and they seemed light, not at all bothered by the sad facts he'd just stated. "It wasn't too bad. Probably not the horror story most people imagine when they think of foster care. I just got moved around a lot and never really made too many connections."

"Well, now you have the family you've been dragged into. I think you've been part of it longer than I have." Shane had known Jack and Luella for a few years and slowly met Evie and Jameson through mutual get-togethers. "If anything, I'm the interloper."

"Nah. They love you, Mini MacCabe."

"Well, thank you. They care about you too. Especially Jack. I swear the way he talks about you, if he swung the other way, you'd be his top choice."

Shane chuckled and rewarded me with a small smile. "Yeah, Jack and I have a pretty strong bond. He's like a brother to me."

"You can have him for a brother. He's just a pain for me."

He laughed again before taking another drink. "How's it going at your job? Was it worth the move? You liking the lab work at the department?"

"Yeah. Getting some breathing room to be myself was worth the move. I love working at the department. There are some terrific people there. And my job at the university is great. I love the work, and I love my lab partner. I just hate my boss."

"Most bosses will ruin it for you."

"He's such a degrading asshole. Doubts Jolene and I every step of the way, and micromanages everything. Like no woman could handle actual science."

Shane laughed at my irritated growl. "I had a boss like that in high school. Of course, I worked at a landscaping company, and I didn't go through years of schooling for it, but he was a real dick. Used to stand over me every time I'd start a weed eater, thinking I was going to break his precious equipment even after three years. Called me out on every mistake and had me write down the time it took to do each job. Like forty-seven minutes to mow the grass. Twenty-eight minutes to edge the yard. Annoying as fuck."

"Exactly. Finally, someone gets it." I threw my hands up in exaggerated celebration before bringing one down on his shoulder. "You get me, Shane."

It took a minute for the heat of his body to seep into my hand. I almost pulled away when I felt it bunch up. But I left it there and swallowed hard when I noticed the way he was staring at my mouth that was so much closer since I'd leaned into him. This was it. This was the moment I'd been waiting for and my mind hadn't even had the time to imagine all the possibilities.

I shifted my legs, bumping them into his, and licked my lips. He leaned fractionally closer to me and my hand slid toward his neck. My heart pumped so loud, I was sure he could hear it. It became the only thing I heard vibrating through the silence of the moment. That and my panting breaths slipping past my lips. His tongue slicked out across his bottom lip, and I focused all my attention on tasting it.

His gaze flicked down to my chest, and I followed his stare to see my nipples pebbled against the material of his shirt. That wouldn't have been such a big deal if I hadn't gotten so turned on. But I liked that he stared. I wanted him to see what he did to me. I leaned in a fraction more and focused on my prize. Just an inch closer and I'd feel his lips claiming me again.

Eeerrrrrrr!

I jumped at the sound and let out a surprised screech, almost falling off my stool. My hand slapped my chest to calm my racing heart.

"Sorry. That's the buzzer for the dryer."

I giggled at how much it had shocked me and he laughed along with me. I looked up at his smiling eyes, the moment broken. "I guess that's my cue to leave."

"I'll drive you home."

"Thank you."

I grabbed my clothes and headed to the bedroom to change. When I strolled out he stood by the door, shrugging on his coat. He looked me up and down and laughed. Well, that isn't promising.

"What?"

"Nice shirt, Mini MacCabe."

I looked down and read it. *Dear NASA, Your mom thought I was big enough. -Pluto*

I laughed along with him. It was one of my favorites. "I collect science T-shirts. The funnier the better."

"I approve, Mini MacCabe. Especially when they fit you so well."

Chapter Ten

Turned out, poor Betsy needed a new fuel pump. I had no idea what that was and nodded blindly as they explained it to me. The part itself wasn't too bad, however the cost of labor had my eyes bugging out. I swore that every time I went to a mechanic shop, they saw "dumb" written on my forehead. *Oh, there's a unicorn poking holes in my tailpipe? Sounds legit. How much will that cost? My first born and a kidney? Good, good. I was going to suggest that as a good price.*

Thankfully, Shane was kind enough to hold my hand and make sure I wasn't getting screwed over for the imaginary unicorn fucking me over. He'd been great all week. On the days I worked at the station, if he was there too, he would give me a ride home. It saved Jolene from having to pick me up. He was different around me at the station. He was . . .Nice.

At least, nice-*er*. He still made fun of me and grumbled at lunch with everyone, but his jokes were no longer mean and snide. They were more sarcastic, but with the intention of making me laugh. Yesterday at lunch, I'd mentioned my date, and everyone chimed in on what I should wear.

Laney said I should show up in nothing but a smile and Shane had grumbled something about a potato sack. When I'd turned to him with a challenging eyebrow raised, I asked if I could message him some ideas because he was my new dating sensei. He'd stared hard at me for a moment before uttering 'sure' and stuffing half of his sandwich in his mouth.

Which brought me to my current situation. I stood in front of my full-length mirror on a Friday night trying to decide what to wear on my date. I looked over my slacks, flats, button-up shirt and cardigan, trying to find the best angle to take a picture. Once I'd settled on a decent one, I sent it off to Shane with a bunch of questions marks.

Shane: Alright grandma.
Me: What???
Shane: I mean, does he have a grandma fetish? Is that why you decided to dress like that?

I rolled my eyes, tossed my phone on the bed, and stomped into my closet for another outfit. The next one consisted of a short floral dress. I figured the exposed thigh would be a win. Then I threw my oversized button up sweater over it. I saw it on Pinterest and thought it looked cute. I took the picture, making sure to show off how short the dress was, and hit send.

Shane: Ohhh. I see.
Shane: He has a hippie grandma fetish.
Me: You're not funny.
Shane: I'm fucking hilarious.

Looking down at myself, I growled into my chest. I didn't

know why I'd decided to ask his opinion. I didn't know what the hell he was hoping I wore, or what a guy liked to see on a woman, but as I pulled my dress over my head, I was tempted to just go with Laney's suggestion of nothing but a smile. With my lips pursed in frustration, I looked at my reflection in the mirror, wearing my black bra and silk panties.

An idea hit me, and my lips lifted into a slow smile, stretching bigger the more I thought about it. I didn't know what possessed me. Maybe the frustration at all the failed dates mixed with the dread I already felt for this date. Especially since Shane had made fun of everything I'd suggested I wear. Whatever it was, I'd reached my limit, and I was going to extract some of my own torture.

Laughing, I dug in the back of my drawer for the sexy lingerie I'd bought online after a bottle of wine. I'd had it for a while, but had never worn it. I stripped off my underwear and bra and slipped on the wisp of black lace that was practically transparent, except for heavier lace covering the nipples. Next came the panties, two strings that wrapped around my hips and left a lace triangle covering between my legs. To top it all off, I slid the garter and stockings on. I pulled my hair down and tousled it until I had that just fucked look.

It took a few tries, but I finally settled on a picture of me with hip cocked and slightly turned, the phone covering my face. Biting my lip, I thought about the repercussions. Fuck it. I hit send. This time it took him forever to reply. I had to triple-check to make sure I actually sent it to him and hadn't accidentally opened up another chat. But when he did respond, I had to laugh. My heart pumped at the banter we had going on, the excitement coursing through my veins bringing a warm flush to my cheeks. All from one word.

Shane: Careful.

Me: Why? I'm just a little girl who probably looks "cute." What do you care?

Shane: I'm still a man and you're playing with fire, Juliana.

Me: I've already tested you out and you were okay. So, I'm good. I don't need to play with you.

Shane: Okay?

Shane: OKAY??

Me: Yup.

I laughed and tossed the phone aside. Checking the time, I needed to hurry if I was going to make my date on time. When I heard my phone ringing, I rushed out of my closet and picked it up.

"Juliana." His deep voice rumbled through the phone and stretched to my core. I had to squeeze my thighs together he sounded so hot. As much as I wanted to give in to the heat between my legs, I kept remembering the way he scolded me in the hallway at Jack's. I couldn't let him get away with being irritated or acting like he was bothered by my body when in reality, his pride had a boo-boo from me telling him he was just "okay."

"You know, Shane. Your pride makes you want to prove you have the biggest, best-working dick. But because of that pride, you seem to forget you think of me as a child who can't handle you."

"It's not my pride that makes me *know* I have the best working dick." I waited for him to acknowledge the fact that he called me a child, but it never came. "I seem to remember four-no five-times you came on my fingers, my tongue, my cock."

I pulled air as far into my lung as possible. His words were making it hard to focus and I needed more oxygen flowing through my body. Letting out my breath, I answered as flippantly as I could.

"Like I said, it was okay."

"I'll show you—"

I hung up before he could respond, a giggle the only sound filling the room once the call was ended. Then my phone chimed in my hand.

Shane: I can't believe you hung up on me. You're damn brave, Mini MacCabe.

I didn't respond, letting him simmer on being called "okay" and then me hanging up on him.

Shane: You're running scared since I reminded you how much better than okay I was at making you scream.

Oh, I didn't need reminding. I was never the one to ignore everything that happened. I was the one who still woke up sweating. I was the one who had trouble breathing when I remembered the ways he had made me scream. How he'd pushed me against the wall in the shower and fell to his knees, never letting his eyes stray from mine. The way he'd dragged his palms up the inside of my thighs until he pushed two fingers roughly inside me. The way he'd propped my thigh on his shoulder and ate my pussy like a starving man. How he pushed me to the brink, just to back off. By the end, I'd had my grip firmly in his hair and began rubbing my cunt against his tongue, threatening his life if he pulled away again.

Oh yeah, I remembered everything.

I swallowed hard and put on a skater skirt and blouse with heels. But before I left, I laid out one more outfit, a leather skirt, thigh high boots, and a skimpy halter top, and took a picture to send to Shane.

Me: I'll wear this then with my lingerie. Hopefully it's not too grandmotherly for my date.

Chapter Eleven

As soon as I got to my car, I jerked the door open and fell into my seat, slamming it behind me.

The date was a bust. And I'm going to warn Jo to never trust the friend who set me up on this date again. The guy was shorter than me, which wasn't a big issue except he used the height difference to stare at my boobs the whole time. On top of that, he had acne, greasy hair, and called me babe all night.

At one point, I tried to salvage the night and made a joke about how my eyes were up higher. His response? To laugh and say, "Babe. Your face is great and all, but those breasts keep calling my name."

Needless to say, I dropped a twenty on the table and got the hell out of there. I looked down at my top. I hadn't even worn anything sexy. Just my skirt and blouse. I'd kept the lingerie on because it made me feel sexy, and maybe I'd hoped to share it with someone, but that was a pipe dream.

So, there I sat, in my cold car, gripping the steering wheel in frustration. I thought of the past month of disastrous dates. Of my frustration with Shane. It built and built until I almost choked on it. Who had this kind of luck? Me. I did.

I heard the voices of Hudson and my parents bouncing around in my head, reminding me I shouldn't be on my own. My frustration bubbled up and boiled over. Letting it out, I growled and screamed as I shook the steering wheel, which only shook me instead.

Done with my fit, I panted heavily, my hair falling in waves over my face. Shane would probably laugh. Say he was right. Ugh. I smacked the wheel for good measure.

Shane. Shane. Shane.

An idea hit me, and maybe because I was just in a 'fuck it' kind of mood, it sounded like the best idea I'd had. I laughed at how crazy it was. But right then, I felt a little crazy.

In the dark of the parking lot, the dome light of my car off, I shrugged out of my long coat. I unzipped my skirt and tugged it off, tossing it in the passenger seat. Then went the blouse before I pulled my coat back on and buttoned it. A pair of wild blue eyes caught my attention in the rear-view mirror and I wondered for a moment if I should bail.

My lips twitched before curving up. I put my keys in Betsy's ignition and went for it. I didn't even turn on music, just let my excited breathing mix with the rumbling of the engine. I sat in the silence and let my imagination flow. Each fantasy better than the last, but I'd hoped, for once, reality was going to top my imagination.

I parked on the street and got out of my car, pulling the coat tighter, highly aware of the way it brushed against the skin of my thighs, bare above the stockings I still wore. The way the material was abrasive against the bare skin of my stomach and ass.

I paused for a moment, my fist hovering above the door, and considered turning around. But I didn't. I rapped my knuckles three times and waited.

Shane opened the door bare chested in a pair of sweats that hung low on his hips. He chuckled at finding me on the other side of his door, and caused me to drag my eyes up from the deep V on either side of his hips.

"Another little date gone wrong, Mini MacCabe? Did he actually have a grandma fetish and was disappointed there were no cardigans? I bet he was even more sad not to have seen those thigh-high boots."

I barely heard him over the blood pounding in my ears, my heart working overtime, fueled by adrenaline and frustration. Either way, I didn't acknowledge it. I only raised my eyebrow and began unbuttoning my coat, slowly, as I held his icy gaze.

The humor that had glinted there a moment before, faded, replaced by a warm heat that followed my fingers from button to button. He was nervous and I liked it. I liked the way his grip tightened on the door. I liked the way his Adam's apple bobbed with a heavy swallow. I liked the way his chest moved a little bit faster.

Once I worked the last button free, I let my coat hang open, exposing the lingerie I was wearing in the picture I'd sent to him earlier.

"Remind me how much better than okay you think you are." He didn't respond, but didn't slam the door in my face either, so I placed my palm against the wood and pushed it open a little more, stepping inside. "Or are you scared that I might be right?" Another step. Noticing the bulge growing in his sweats, I took the tip of my finger and dragged it along the length, all the way from root to tip. "That you really are. Just. Okay."

Lightning fast, his hand shackled tightly around the wrist of the hand currently taunting his dick.

"You want to play with me, little girl?" He tugged, pulling me into his chest, skin to skin, so hot I wanted to melt. "You want me to teach you what it feels like to be fucked by a man, unlike those boys who don't know what to do with this tight pussy?"

"Yes, sir." The answer barely slipped past my lips on a breath before he slammed the door shut behind me. "Teach me."

He looked me over like he didn't know where to start first. The anticipation, watching his hand clench and unclench next to his leg, like he was holding back was the best kind of torture. Standing before him like this, was so much different than the night in Jamaica. I'd surprised him, snuck into his room and he took me. Over and over, but there was no hesitation, no words of denial between us like there was now.

This tonight, was a whole new experience I was practically panting to start.

His hand finally relaxed and brushed the coat aside, dragging his calloused fingertips up my inner thigh until they reached the wet panties covering my core. He gently stroked back and forth, not saying anything, letting the tension build before he pushed the edge aside and slipped between the lips of my pussy and played in the wetness, teasing my cunt. Not entering, not stroking hard enough to push me over the edge. Just touching and spreading my juices all around as he looked me up and down.

He moved to my clit and I cried out when he pinched it in between his fingers. "You're going to fall to your knees, and suck my cock."

A part of me almost caved right then and there, my mouth watering at the thought of tasting him again. But as much as I wanted him to teach me, I wanted him to know that I wasn't quite the little girl he assumed I was.

So, I laughed. Right in his face, enjoying the way his eyes widened at my response.

I rolled my hips, trying to gain some friction between my legs beyond the punishing grip he had on my bud. "How about *you* fall to *your* knees and get your face between my legs."

He breathed out a laugh that brushed against my lips before he released my clit and gripped the flimsy lace, tearing them from my body. I yelped, unprepared for the sting cutting into my skin.

His eyes never left mine as he dropped slowly to his knees and parted my lips. He stroked his tongue from my opening to the top. He held my eyes right up until he plunged his tongue inside me and my eyes fell closed in pleasure.

He left no part of my pussy untasted. I reached my arm behind me to try and find the wall for support, but we were too far away, planted in the middle of his entryway, him on his knees worshiping my core with his mouth, me clinging to his shoulders for support, fighting from tumbling over top of him.

My nails dug into his muscles and the buzzing in my ears grew louder. My toes curled in the pumps I still wore, trying to find purchase on the ground before I floated away. He pushed me over the edge when he shoved two fingers inside me and flicked his tongue in fast strokes across my bundle of nerves, wrenching cries of pleasure from my throat.

Once I'd finally came down from my orgasm, he placed one last kiss to my pussy and stood, dragging his body up mine, stopping to bite at my hard nipples. Continuing until he stood before me and planted his lips on mine, shoving his tongue inside, making me taste myself. He pulled back and stared at me as he walked backward toward his couch. Then he sat, his legs wide.

As I shrugged off my coat, letting it fall to the floor, he tugged his pants down enough to free his long, thick dick. Stretching one arm along the back of the couch, he watched my approach and began stroking himself. I couldn't help but stare at the way his fingers gripped his shaft and slowly glided up and down.

"*Now* you will get over here and suck my dick."

He didn't have to ask. I wanted nothing more than to lay at his feet and taste him. I set about remembering every groove, vein, and hidden flavor of him. I sucked the head of him soft, like a lollipop before I dove down as far as I could, pushing past my gag reflex, loving the way he moaned and his hand tightened in my hair. Loving the way his other hand reached down my body and pushed my bra out of the way so he could play with my nipples. Roll them around in his thick fingers.

I picked up my pace, wanting to make him come, wanting to swallow all of it, when he tugged hard at my hair, removing my mouth from his dick with a pop. I looked up, confused as to why he stopped me.

"Turn around, but stay on your knees."

I did as he instructed and faced a wooden coffee table. He slid from the couch to his knees behind me and placed a hand between my shoulder blades, pushing me down until I lay across the cold tabletop.

"These garters are fucking torture. Like you're wearing clothes, and yet your perfect pussy is exposed, begging me to fuck it."

"Yes," I moaned.

He reached in a drawer beside me and extracted a condom. I heard the crinkle and waited with anticipation for that first push. Would it be slow? Fast? Hard? Soft?

His hand moved back to the spot on my back, holding me firm to the table as his other hand moved his dick to my opening. He swiped it up and down my juices, smacking against my clit a couple of times before he lined himself up and shoved in all at once. His deep groan of pleasure mixed with my cry of pain. It'd been so long and he was so big. But he didn't stop. He pulled out, all the way before he did it again. And again. The pinch each time burning and flowing throughout my body, morphing into pleasure.

The edge of the table dug into my stomach on each thrust. My nipples rubbed against the cold wood. My body jerked with his forceful thrusts. It was painful. It was wonderful.

He moved a hand and gripped a fistful of my hair and jerked my head up, bending my neck so he could lean down and whisper in my ear as he fucked me.

"Little girl." Each time the name slipped past his lips, it made me feel dirty and wrong. And I loved it. I loved the way he controlled me and owned me. "Is this what you wanted me to teach you? To teach this tight cunt what it feels like to be stretched. What it feels like to hurt and to like it."

Tears leaked out of the corner of my eyes from the burn of him pulling my hair. "Yes. Yes." The words were quiet cries. Quiet pleas to never stop.

He pushed in and pulled the top of my body off the table, it arched away from him with my head pulled back into his chest. He pounded into me over and over, grunts mixing with the sound of our flesh smacking together. He reached around and toyed with my nipples, switching from one to the other, dragging me to the brink.

"Shane. Please. Shane." My words were incoherent and when he pinched my nipple hard, the fiery burn set me off and I came, my cries unable to be hidden with how I was exposed. They flew into the room with abandon, getting louder with each rippling wave of pleasure, soon to be mixed with his groans.

When we both finished, he loosened his hold on my hair and I collapsed back to the table, where he slowly pulled out of me and disposed of the condom. I let myself slide to the floor and laid back, staring at the ceiling, until he came back to stand above me. He'd lost his pants and he looked so proud, strong, and unabashed with his dick hanging thick and heavy above me, nothing hidden from view.

Smiling, I rose from my spot on the floor and stared into his eyes, trying to find what he was thinking. Shaking my head, I turned to grab my coat and leave, minus a pair of panties. But he stopped me with a hand to my jaw and a questioning look.

"I should go."

He didn't move, just his eyes taking me in as though pondering what to do next. I fully expected him to let go of me and help

me gather my things. It was Shane after all, I didn't expect anything more when I came here.

But he did none of that. Instead, he chuckled, letting go of
my jaw, dragging his fingers down my body to between my legs.
I gasped when he hooked two fingers inside my pussy and began
walking backward toward the hallway. I followed him. He was
literally dragging me around his apartment by my pussy. And I
loved it.

"Oh, no, Mini MacCabe. You're mine for the night. And next
time, you're going to swallow my cum."

Chapter Twelve

The sun hit my eyes first.

Then the memories of the previous night.

Then the heavy arm wrapped around my waist and the thick head pushing at the entrance of my pussy. It slipped in my already wet opening. With a hand gripped around my breast to hold me in place, it pushed back in all the way to the hilt.

I turned my head just enough to bury it in the pillow and groan.

"Don't hide your pleasure from me. You know how much I love to hear you." Shane's morning voice may have been hotter than his usual one. Just a little gruffer. Mixed with the way he nibbled my earlobe and licked his way down my neck as he worked himself in an out of me first thing in the morning, this was shaping up to be the best day of my life.

I tipped my hips back to give him more access and everything felt so slick and wet and bare.

Bare. Fuck.

"Shane." I breathed his name on a sharp thrust. "Condom."

He picked up his pace before holding himself inside me, and I wasn't sure he'd even heard me.

"I'm clean." He grumbled in my ear, like it solved all our problems. "I've never been in a pussy bare before. So fucking hot. Wet. So fucking good."

My core tightened around him, loving his words and knowing I was clean too. But still.

"I'm not on birth control."

That made him pause for a solid second before he pushed back in and continued his slow but hard pace.

"Then I'll be sure to come on your tits."

Pushing myself back onto him, grinding against his cock, hoping I was coating his balls with my juices, I gave him permission to continue. It may have been reckless, but I trusted him to pull out.

His pace picked up and I tried to pinch my thighs together to get more friction on my clit, but it wasn't enough. I moved my hand between my thighs and started rubbing fast circles over my nub. I was so close.

"That's it baby. Use my cock to get off. Touch yourself."

His movements lost any rhythm and he frantically pounded in and out of me, pinching my nipple in the process.

"Come, Juliana. Come." He rolled my nipple and I focused on pushing back against him, rubbing faster and faster until my eyes slammed shut and my mouth fell open as I came.

I hadn't even finished before he jerked his dick out of me and flipped me to my back. Shane rose to his knees and jerked his cock hard and fast. I watched in fascination, still rubbing my clit and riding my orgasm as he fell over me, the muscles in the arm supporting his weight strained as he groaned and released cum all over my breasts.

"Fuck," he breathed, staring down at all the white ropes spread across my curves up to my neck. His chest heaved as he used his thumb to swipe a drop of cum off my nipple. He moved his hand to my mouth and pushed it in as he lowered his head and sucked the residual come off my puckered tip.

So fucking hot. A man not put off by his own taste. The same taste that was exploding on my tongue, salty and warm. I squeezed my legs together, still feeling the throb in my core.

With one last kiss to my nipple, Shane pulled back and stood from the bed, completely unashamed of his nudity. Not that he had a reason with his broad chest, abs, and the most beautiful dick hanging between two muscular legs. He was gorgeous.

I, however, waited until he walked through his bathroom door and then wiped the excess cum off my body with a tissue and wrapped the sheet around me to follow him. By the time I walked in, the shower was on and the room was steamy. Should I have dropped the sheet and joined him? Was that what he wanted? Or was I supposed to sit on the bed and wait my turn? Or, even worse, was I supposed to be gone by the time he got out. Most importantly, why hadn't he kicked me out last night?

My head jerked from side to side from the shower to the door. Then I remembered how he'd literally dragged me around by my pussy. *Fuck it.* I dropped the sheet and entered the shower with him.

He slicked his hair back under the water and looked me over with a smirk. "'Bout time."

I didn't know what to say, so I settled on rolling my eyes at him. He laughed at my childish response and jerked his chin, indicating behind me. "You can use my shampoo and soap. Sorry I don't have any fancy conditioner or whatever the hell else you ladies use."

"These will do, thank you."

I washed my hair and we rotated so I could rinse off. When I turned back around, he had a loofah already lathered with soap and tugged me out from under the spray to start washing my body. He used his bare hands to wash between my legs and took extra time on my breasts.

"Do you want me to clean you?" I asked, letting my eyes lower to between his legs.

"Hell, yes. But just clean, Mini MacCabe. I'm not young enough to get it up that quickly, like all those other boys you've been with."

He laughed and said the words like he assumed I had a harem of men waiting for me in Texas. And why wouldn't he since he'd seen me go on countless dates.

I didn't know what the hell pushed me to admit it, but before I could stop myself, the words tumbled from my lips. "I've only had sex with two other people."

The loofah froze between us as he let my words sink in, not moving. The silence stretched and hung between us for what seemed like an hour, but was probably less than a minute.

"It makes me feel like a caveman for how much that pleases me."

I chuckled at his admission. "Well, whatever you feel, I like it."

"Good." He smirked. "Now be a good girl and wash me up."

I cocked my eyebrow at his demand, but took the loofah and began rubbing him down. He jerked when my fingers grazed his sides and again on his inner thigh.

"Is the big, strong, impenetrable wall, known as Shane . . .Ticklish?" I mock gasped and placed my hand across my chest.

"No."

He went to grab the loofah back to finish the job, but I pulled back and laughed at him, using my free hand to poke at his ribs. This turned into a very slippery tickle fight, and I was exhausted by the time the water ran cold, which forced us to quickly rinse off and exit the shower.

"How about I make breakfast while you get dressed," Shane suggested as he wrapped the towel around his waist.

"About that, can I borrow something to wear? I didn't completely think through only arriving in lingerie, and my clothes are in my car. Also, someone ruined my panties."

"Such a shame about that." He tsked and shook his head with a small smile. "Looks like you're not so brave in the morning, huh."

I gave him a pointed stare, telling him I didn't find him funny in the least. He leaned in to kiss my pursed lips and pulled back quickly.

"I'll leave some stuff on the bed."

Once he left, I helped myself to his toothpaste, using my finger to clean my teeth, and headed to the bedroom. I went to grab the white shirt on his bed, when I saw my reflection in the mirror of his dresser. Dropping the towel, I looked at myself and tried to see what Shane did. My breasts were smaller, barely a C-cup. I was tall and skinny, but muscular from working out. I didn't have many curves and it made me feel self-conscious. But remembering the heat in Shane's eyes when he took me, made me look at myself differently. It made me see a woman that an older man, who's most likely experienced all kinds of women, enjoyed.

Taking a deep breath, I smiled and grabbed the shirt and long lounge pants that would have to suffice.

When I walked out to the living room, a smile firmly planted on my face, I hadn't expected to find a scowling Shane. He directed his glare at me, and I slowed my walk toward him in the kitchen, my smile slipping from my face.

"Didn't realize you were fucking someone else." His words were low and angry.

"Uhhhh . . ." I sounded dumb, but what the hell else was I supposed to say? I stood there with eyes wide, unsure of why I was being reprimanded. "What?"

He tossed something toward me, and it landed on the couch. When I went for it, I saw it was my phone. I pressed my home button to bring the screen to life and saw a message from Hudson.

Hudson: Next time you come home, you can be sure to stay with me. I'm sure we can find ways to avoid your parents and enjoy each other.

The laugh started small over the idea that I would stay with Hudson when I was home. Then as I rolled over Shane's words and realized he thought I was with Hudson, it grew to a full belly laugh. And looking at Shane's curled lip, and the muscle in his jaw flexing, I needed to start explaining.

"Oh, my god. Hudson is my ex-boyfriend who is in cahoots with my parents to get me to come home. We broke up a long time ago and for some reason he thinks after more than a year apart, I'm going realize I made a mistake and go home so we could start our life together."

"And . . .?" Shane looked at me pointedly, waiting for my answer.

A butterfly took flight in my chest at all the reasons why he would be bothered by me seeing my ex-boyfriend.

"And nothing. Hudson is my past. Period."

"Good."

I watched him walk around the island, setting out silverware next to plates filled with eggs, and I had to ask the question that had been on repeat all morning. "Why am I still here?" He froze and lifted his eyes to mine. "I mean, as the consummate bachelor, I figured I'd have been shown the door last night. Now you're here setting the table for a breakfast you made for me. It doesn't quite fit the picture I'd imagined of you."

"Well, Mini MacCabe," he said, standing upright, holding my gaze. "I figured if I was going to have you, then I was going to take as much time as I wanted. If I was going to allow myself to give in to you just this once, then I was going to use every second. The breakfast is purely selfish to keep us both fueled for the next round."

My mind tried to focus on the next round, but it stumbled over his other words. "What do you mean just this once?"

He pinched his lips, letting out a heavy sigh through his nose, and looked at me like a child that needed everything broken down for her. It annoyed me.

"This can't happen again, Mini MacCabe." I cocked an irritated eyebrow and crossed my arms. I liked the way his eyes drew to my breasts' movement. "I'm not going to explain why, because you know." He ran his hand through his hair. "Are we going to do this? Or are we going to refuel and see how much fucking we can fit in today?"

Part of me wanted to have the conversation, but where would it leave me. Walking out the door, without breakfast and more sex? I didn't like that idea at all. And when the practical side of my brain took over, I knew I was spending more time with Shane than I'd originally expected. And maybe I'd come back to the "just this once" comment later. Preferably naked, with him on his knees, mouth at my pussy. My lips tipped up at that image.

"If we're not fucking anymore after this, are you still going to be my friend, or is that a short-term offer too?" I asked, remembering our conversation from the bar. I didn't like the idea of no more sex, but I *hated* the idea of losing his friendship.

"Yes, little girl. I'll still be your friend." His tone was a little mocking of my request, but I'd take it.

"Good. Then I look forward to seeing what you're capable of after breakfast."

He chuckled. "Oh, you will, little girl. Now come eat the scrambled eggs I made you before I decide to bend you over the table and spank you."

"But what if I've been a bad girl?" I gave him a doe-eyed look.

He barked out a laugh and pulled out my stool. When I sat, he leaned in over my shoulder and spoke softly in my ear. "There is no 'if' about you being a bad girl. You are. And, don't worry, I'll turn your ass cherry red later. And afterward you can suck my cock again to make up for how bad you've been." He pulled back and swatted the side of my bottom, causing me to yelp. "Now eat up. We have a *busy* afternoon."

Chapter Thirteen

"Well, well, well," Jolene greeted me when I entered our apartment. "Look who finally decided to show up, and wearing the same damn thing as last night." She turned on the couch to look me over with a proud smile. "I'll make sure to have my friend set me up with a guy next."

"What about the guy you've been seeing?" I dropped my purse and coat in the entryway and leaned my hip against the arm of the couch.

"Meh. Old news."

"Well, don't get your hopes up. Last night's date was a disgusting pig. And I didn't even get to finish my dinner before I walked out on him."

"Ummm . . .Okay." She looked me over again, probably trying to find hints of why I was still wearing last night's clothes if not for my date. "So, what's with the walk of shame?"

"Oh, Jo." I heaved a deep breath. "Let me shower while you

order us Chinese. I'll tell you all about it after I get some new clothes on."

"It better be good." She pointed at me with narrowed eyes as she headed to the kitchen.

I showered quickly, but stopped to look at my reflection in the mirror, smiling at the small bite mark Shane had left on my inner thigh after breakfast, when he'd had me for dessert on the kitchen island. I clenched my core before grabbing lounge pants and a tank top.

When I came out, Jo had an obscene amount of takeout containers spread out and my stomach rumbled. I'd worked up a hell of an appetite last night.

"Mmm." I moaned my approval and loaded up my plate, ignoring Jo's pointed stare.

"Okay, you have your Lo Mein and egg roll. Now spill." She pointed her chopsticks at me with narrowed eyes, and I quickly swallowed my first bite so I could divulge my evening.

"After the date from hell, I was so frustrated and in a 'fuck it' kind of mood."

"I think we both live in a perpetual 'fuck it' kind of mood. But continue."

I nodded at her assessment, but moved on, knowing the next part was going to garner a big reaction.

"I showed up at Shane's in just my underwear and my coat, and I stripped in front of him, demanding he sleep with me." It all poured out in a rush, escaping in one breath.

I wasn't disappointed as her eyes rounded and her jaw dropped. "Oh, fuck *yes* you did." Jo held her hand up for a high five and a smile split across her face. I laughed and slapped my hand to hers. "Details. Now."

I broke down our night, skimming over the sex. Blushing and smiling the whole time. My heart fluttered with each word and I giggled throughout the conversation as if I was the little girl Shane accused me of being.

"You stayed the night?" Jo asked with wide eyes.

"Obviously."

"And he cooked you breakfast?"

"Yup."

"So, what? Does this mean you guys are together?"

My shoulders dropped and I paused for a minute, thinking it over. "No. He said it was the only time, even though I think he wants more." I answered honestly. "He did get upset over a message from Hudson that implied we were together. But I think that had more to do with his pride than feeling possessive of me."

"What about you? Do you want more?"

A laugh burst out of me. "Of course. God, he makes me feel amazing." I closed my eyes and took a deep breath before letting it out and looking at Jo. "But even if it was the only time, it was worth it. Soooo worth it."

"As long as you're okay with it, then I say get you some." She shimmied and I laughed at her encouragement.

"He's worried about our age difference. And then there is Jack. I think a lot of things play into whether I can 'get me some' after last night. I haven't given up just yet."

"Whatever." She waved her hand holding the chopsticks. "I think it's hot. He knows a lot more than younger men. So, just enjoy it and see where it goes."

"Cheers to that."

We tapped chopsticks and dug into our food.

Sunday brunch was stressful. I tried to hold onto the aloofness I felt with Jo last night, but sitting across the table from Shane, made it hard to focus. Add the fact that Shane barely acknowledged me, hardly even made eye contact. Let's just say I was frustrated.

"How's work at the station," Jack asked Shane when we'd all gathered around the table.

"Good. Busy. Been pulled out on call a lot. I may need to get with you on a certain case."

"Yeah? Swing by the office any time." Jack took a drink before cocking an eyebrow at Shane. "You at the station enough to keep an eye on my little sister?"

I ground my jaw as my brother flawlessly cock-blocked me, by reminding Shane of my position in Jack's life. *Little sister.* I was beginning to hate those two words.

"I wouldn't want to have to go to the station and kick any guy's ass who was hitting on Juliana."

Jack laughed like he was the next Lewis Black. Shane laughed awkwardly before taking long pulls of his beer. I was about to roll my eyes when I caught Evie's pointed stare and smirk. I looked away, but couldn't ignore her knowing look. She was too perceptive for her own good.

She knew. And if she knew, then Lu would know. And if Lu would know then Jack would know. And if Jack would know, Shane would never come within one hundred feet of me. My body wept over the possible loss.

It all gave me such a headache, so when lunch was over and the bar opened for business, I plopped myself on a stool and asked for a double vodka cranberry.

I was only one in before the inevitable happened, and Evie slid up next to me. I refused to look her way. She could stare me down all day, but I was going to stare into my drink like it held the outcomes of my future. Unfortunately, she wasn't deterred by my silence.

"Not gonna lie, Shane was not the Popsicle I expected you to suck on."

Her drink arrived and while she sipped, I begrudgingly looked over at her. With the glass still to her lips, she winked at me. Taunting me.

"How?" I needed to know what she saw that gave me away, so I didn't do it again. "How do you know?"

She shrugged. "I'm more observant than you think. As much as you stared at Shane and as much as he refused to look at you, I could put two and two together."

"Does anyone else know?"

"Nah. The boys are oblivious. Luella may have picked up on it, but she's no snitch."

My shoulders slouched and I sipped from the tiny straw until all the red was gone from my glass. Jameson was down on the other side of the bar, laughing with an employee. Jack and Lu had gone home, and so had Shane.

I looked over at Evie again. *Fuck it.* Taking a chance on having another confidant, I spilled the beans.

"I slept with Shane in Jamaica."

She let out a mock gasp and brought her hand to her chest. "What? Really? I'm flabbergasted."

"Shut up."

"You guys were all over each other, and his early departure and your moping afterward was a dead giveaway. But once again, I'm more observant than you'd think."

Digging both hands into my hair, I told her everything. About my hopes and how he'd squashed them. About the frustration of shitty dates and how I'd channeled that into seducing Shane and about how I'd succeeded. Then I spilled the issues: Jack and my age.

"Jack is not your keeper. And you're young. Just because you fuck someone, doesn't mean you are going to marry him. So, enjoy him and let him teach you the tricks of the trade."

"He said that night was a one-time deal. I didn't push it at the time, because it's Shane and I didn't expect more. But I'm not going to lie and say I don't think about it all the time. And after the way he acted at brunch today, I'm surprised if he even wants to talk to me again."

"That's because Jack was there. Be bold, Juliana. Be brave. Go talk to him and see what he wants. Better yet, show him what he wants."

I wanted to. I wanted to *bad*. Ordering a water, I took a moment to imagine the possibilities. A repeat of what happened outside the bathroom at Jack's could happen. I could get mad again, but at least know I tried. I could *not* go to him and then always wonder. Or I could go to him, demand he take me like I did the other night and continue to have ridiculously fabulous orgasms.

The last possibility was the scariest, but had the best rewards. I chugged my water before dropping a twenty on the bar and left to go show Shane what he wanted.

By the time I arrived, my nerves were trying to kick in. I gave myself a pep-talk and shook out my arms and walked up to his door, knocking with authority.

As soon as he opened the door, his eyes flashed with heat followed quickly by regret. I ignored the regret.

"Juliana, I don't think we should do this."

"Why?" Such a simple question I wanted him to answer. Maybe if he said it out loud he would realize how wrong he was.

I pushed past him into his apartment and he closed the door while I waited for him to explain.

"I'm older than you."

"And yet, you're the one letting someone tell you what you can't do."

My comment hit its mark and his jaw clenched. I gestured for him to continue his reasons as I made myself comfortable, lounging back on his couch.

"My job isn't conducive to having relationships. I'm busy. It's dangerous. I'm unreliable. It pisses women off, and I can't commit to anything."

"Am I asking you to?" I smirked at his hands clenching and unclenching by his side, knowing how hard he had to fight to hold himself back.

"Jack is my best friend—my brother. He'd kill me if he knew what I've done to you."

I held his stare, pulling a Sharon Stone, crossing and uncrossing my legs. I wore pants, but the way his eyes dropped, I knew I'd drawn his attention where I wanted it.

"What I still want to do to you." His response rumbled across the room and vibrated across my skin.

Licking my lips, knowing I was about to get my way, I asked, "And what do you still want to do to me?"

He hesitated but finally opened his mouth to respond, and my phone beeped with an incoming text. I wanted to ignore it, but then it beeped again.

He cocked an eyebrow, waiting for me to grab my phone, but I sat there, holding his challenging gaze, delivering one of my own. But when my phone began ringing, I heaved a sigh and grabbed it from my purse.

I saw Jolene's name on the screen just before the ringing stopped. I hadn't got to it on time. Not that it mattered because a moment later, it began ringing again.

"Hey," I answered, glaring at Shane.

"I'm an idiot and locked myself out. Is there any way you could come let me in? Pleeeeease."

"How did you lock yourself out?"

"There was this guy in the hall who distracted me."

I rolled my eyes but chuckled at how she probably got *distracted*. Leaning down, I grabbed my purse and then stood. "I'm on my way."

"Thank you, thank you, thank you."

I dropped my phone back in my bag and met Shane's relieved eyes. We didn't say anything, just stared at each other in the middle of the apartment waiting the other one out. For what, I didn't know. However, he won the staring contest, using his detective skills to mask his emotions.

I couldn't help but chuckle at how stubborn he was and shook my head before making my way to the door. As I walked past, I made sure to brush his arm and take note of his still clenching fists. Mr. Detective couldn't mask all his feelings.

Once I reached the door, I paused with my hand on the knob before looking back over my shoulder. "He doesn't have to know what happens between us."

"Juliana."

One word. Growled out from a man who sounded close to breaking, but too stubborn to give in. I wanted to push, but I needed to get to Jolene.

"One day, Shane," I promised. Then I opened the door and closed it softly behind me.

One day, I'd wear him down. Maybe not today or tomorrow, but I knew what I wanted and as much as he tried to deny it and hide it, I knew he wanted it, too.

Chapter Fourteen

"Happy Birthday!" Everyone raised their glass and shouted in unison, smiling at the grumbly birthday boy.

"I hate celebrating my birthday." Shane flattened his mouth and stared everyone down before begrudgingly saying thank you, and drinking from his beer with everyone else.

"It's because you're getting to be an old man." Jack joked and slapped Shane's back in good fun. I couldn't help but notice the way his eyes flicked to me, before jerking away and taking another long pull from his beer.

It had been two weeks since I'd stopped by his apartment. I hadn't been back for a few reasons: one, because I'd been busy, and two, as much as I hated to admit it, I was nervous about being turned down again.

Also, I was really enjoying torturing him at the station when we were both there. Wearing lower-cut shirts and being sure to lean forward enough so he could get a glimpse of my lacy bra. If we ever crossed paths, I made sure to brush against him, a hand against his arm or his chest.

It seemed after that first week of torture he'd been called out of the station for work more and more. I liked to imagine it was because he couldn't control himself with me. I liked to imagine that if he stayed in the same building, he'd drag me into a closet and finally give in to what we both wanted, yanking my pants down, and roughly fucking me in desperation against a wall. But in reality, I knew it was most likely a case.

One night, we ended up walking out together to our cars. I started mine and looked up to pull out to see him watching me. When he noticed me staring, he jerked his door open and left without another glance back. I smiled, imagining what would happen if he stayed. Maybe he'd have stormed over to my car and pulled me into the back seat to taste me, kiss me, take me. He wouldn't say a word. Just make us both come and leave me an exhausted, satisfied, sweaty mess in the back seat.

We could be so creative in being together without anyone knowing. If only he'd give in already.

Well, Evie and Jolene would know since they already knew. Which meant Luella would eventually know too, but I refused to think about that. Especially with Jo currently giving me a subtle blow job motion as she pointed at Shane, who was talking to my brother. I laughed and itched the side of my head with a middle finger.

We had all gathered at the brand-spanking-new King's to celebrate Shane's birthday. The restaurant had opened last week, and Jameson stood proudly behind the bar with Evie doing her best to distract him with her cleavage. The whole gang was there, including Shane's partner, Reese, and one of my brother's employees, Clark, who kept showing up at events when he knew Jolene would be there. *Interesting.* I'd be sure to give her shit about that later.

Clark actually stared at her and turned to find me watching.

I gave him a raised eyebrow and pursed lips. *I see you, Clark, eyeing my best friend.*

With a smirk and a shrug of his shoulders, he stepped close enough to me so that no one could hear.

"Your friend Jolene single?"

"Maybe." I didn't look up at him, just took another sip of my drink.

"Juliana. Come on, help a guy out."

Shane just happened to turn and his eyes darkened when he noticed Clark's hand on my shoulder. I decided to fuck with him a little.

Eyeing Clark, I arched my back and stuck out my chest. "Why? You gonna be good to her? Or are you just looking for a wham-bam-thank-you-ma'am?"

He threw his head back and laughed, drawing my brother's attention and causing Shane to take a step closer to me.

"Watch it, Clark. That's my baby sister. You better keep your hands, eyes, and thoughts away from her."

Clark stepped back with his hands raised.

"You're such a cock-blocker, Jack."

Jack glared at me, not at all impressed with my loud insult.

"Yeah, Jack," Evie said, cutting in. "Let your sister live a little. She could probably have any man in this place. Except Jameson, of course." She winked at me and gave a slight nod toward Shane. "Come on, Jules. Take your pick. Ask a guy to dance, and I guarantee he'll say yes. And I'll hold Jack's cock-blocking ways back, or I'll end up cock-blocking him tonight." She smirked in my brother's direction and threw her arm around Luella.

"Hmm." Bringing my finger to my lips, I looked around the bar at all the men even though I knew who I was going to settle on. I turned my back on Shane before whipping around and meeting his glaring eyes. "Shane." I loved the way his jaw ticked, holding back his frustration. "Dance with me?"

"Fuck no," Jack said before Shane could answer. "Juliana, Shane doesn't want to dance with my little sister."

His words stung more than I wanted them to and I ground my teeth, letting my brother see my full frustration before turning back to Shane. He was trying to avoid my gaze by looking down to the floor, but kept glancing up at me anyway.

My bravado sunk to the floor along with my stomach. He was going to say no. Everyone stood around watching after Evie talked me up, and the man was going to turn me down. Maybe Jack was right. Maybe Shane didn't want anything to do with his baby sister. Dropping my head, I swallowed the lump forming in my throat. I needed to gather my emotions and stop the blush burning my cheeks.

Just as I was about to lift my head, a phony smile firmly in place to laugh it off, his deep voice reached across the space between us, saving me.

"Sure, Mini MacCabe. I'll dance with you."

"Don't you dare." Jack pointed a finger at him. He was friendly, completely unaware that Shane would actually want me, let alone have already had me.

"I'll treat her nice, Jackie-boy," Shane said, goading Jack. His hand dropped to the top of my head, like a pat before sliding down between my shoulder blades and stepping up behind me, facing Jack, who looked more annoyed and bored at Shane's antics than serious.

Shane would never touch me in a serious way in front of Jack, but I couldn't deny the thrill I felt even when his hand warmed my skin. I couldn't deny the image of him touching me in a way that claimed me. In a way that let everyone know I was his. Instead, it was all a joke. Silly banter between two friends.

Shane guided me to the dance floor and I threw a smile over my shoulder at Jack, just to piss him off. Evie, Lu, and Jo cat-called as we walked away. When we hit the edge of the floor, I stepped in close and rested my hands on his neck, my back to Jack.

"You're a pretty brave man for one who doesn't want to get caught."

"Nah, I just like to heckle Jack. Give him shit."

"Well, it seems to be working." I looked over my shoulder to find Jack glaring at us and Lu and Evie laughing beside him. I stepped closer and let my hands drag down Shane's chest, amping up Jack's irritation.

Shane played along and dropped his big palms low on my back, encroaching on my ass. I wanted to grind on him right there, but he wasn't going too far with Jack and held some distance between us. Even so, the feel of him touching me in public was more intoxicating than I could have imagined.

It'd been a long time since Shane had wrapped me in his arms in public. Ever since Jamaica where we were forced to dance together as the wedding party. He'd stared down at me, letting his eyes graze my chest, exposed by my low-cut bridesmaid dress. I'd asked him if he liked what he saw, and he'd grunted and told me he could appreciate any pair of tits.

It had been a brush off, saying mine were no special than anyone else's, however, when I'd let my hips push into his, I'd felt how much he'd appreciated my small curves. It had been that moment that I'd decided to sneak into his room and seduce him, and that I wouldn't leave Jamaica without at least trying.

The song picked up the beat and I eliminated the distance between us, putting on a show. Shane tried to hold me steady, but took advantage of the torture I was delivering to Jack and playing along a little bit. I'd twirl around Shane, letting my hands glide across his chest, and shimmy close to him, moving my hips against him. I could hear Lu and Evie cheering from the tables off to the side.

The real treat was Shane's laugh. He laughed through it all and it was beautiful. Shane smiled on occasion, but he rarely laughed. I couldn't help but join him and we became two loons laughing on the dance floor. My heart felt so much joy that I thought it would explode.

When a slow song came on, he stopped his antics and just held me close, letting the song fill our silence. Jack had waved us off, thinking all of our exaggerated touches were innocent and just to fuck with him. He was only half right. But standing in the loop of Shane's arms, I had to fight laying my head on his chest and letting my affection for him show.

"Thank you for dancing with me."

"It's not too much of a hardship, Mini MacCabe."

"I know. But I also know you don't want to give Jack any reason to suspect you've defiled me."

His Adam's apple bobbed when I let my hips drift closer to his. Now was my moment to push again and every part of me screamed to make it happen.

"Shane, I know you want this as much as me. And I was serious when I said no one has to know."

"I don't do relationships or commitment. I'm not the man to make promises."

"I'm not asking you to. I'm a woman going after something that makes her feel good. Just sex."

He looked over my head, scanning the crowd as if it would have the answers for the right thing to say. Finally, his gaze landed back on mine, and in it, I saw the crack in his resolve. He was going to give in.

"I'm thirty-eight now. Thirteen years older than you."

I tipped my head back to stare up at him. "You say that like it's a bad thing."

He paused and his eyebrows pinched together. "You're too young to waste time with someone as old as me."

"The way I see it, you've got thirteen more years of experience and things to show me."

His eyes heated to a warm blue. "I do have a lot I want to show you." His words rumbled in his chest, vibrating against my breasts pressed tightly to him, hardening my nipples.

Victory surged through my veins, my heart pumping faster in

excitement. All the memories of the ways he felt inside me and against me poured over my body like lava.

"Why don't you come by my place tonight and teach me something new?"

He hesitated. "Your roommate?" He said it like it was all the reason to never step foot in my apartment.

"I'm a big girl, Shane. I can have sleepovers. And she won't care. She won't tell anyone."

"And if Jack stops by?"

"Jack never comes over." I raised an eyebrow, waiting for his next rebuttal. "Come on, Shane. There's no good reason not to."

He looked down at me with a playful smirk. "I can't promise to be quiet, Mini MacCabe. I want to do a lot of loud things with you, and I sure as hell know you can't be quiet."

I smiled, knowing I was winning him over. "I'll give her earplugs or headphones."

He stared down at my lips and I dragged my tongue across them, slowly to torture him.

"Fuck, I can't wait to get out of here."

"Alright, Shane," Jack called from the table at the edge of the dance floor, breaking the moment. "You're real fucking funny. Now come over here and have another drink with me."

I smirked at Shane before I backed away and we walked to the table. When we got there, I caught Jack's eye before I turned to Shane, blowing him a kiss. "Thanks for the dance."

Then I twirled away and walked toward the bar where Evie greeted me with a high-five.

"You are playing with fire," Luella said. "I think I saw some real sparks there."

I just shrugged and grabbed the drink I'd ordered.

"So, ummm," Luella started, voice lowered. "Are you and Shane together?"

I laughed at her conspiratorial whisper. "No."

"You know I don't have a problem if you are. I just need to

prepare myself for when Jack finds out." She made an explosion sound, spreading her hands wide.

"You don't need to worry about your husband, Lu."

"I'm sure you can find ways to calm him down," Evie said, sliding her hand up and down her tall glass, bobbing her eyebrows.

"Ew. I don't need to know what you and Jack do," I said, cringing.

"Oh, we do lots of things, Jules," Jack interrupted behind me. "You want to pretend to molest my best friend in front of me, I think there's some payback that needs to happen."

I pretended to gag as he pulled Lu into his arms and kissed her long and hard.

Shane joined our group and leaned on the bar next to me, shaking his head at my brother. Just seeing his strong forearm on the wood counter, the way his hands splayed out as he waited for another beer, sent a jolt of excitement down my stomach to my core. I couldn't wait to feel those fingers stroking my skin again.

Glancing at the clock, I saw we had at least another hour before people would start piling out. It was going to be the longest hour of torture, knowing I had to wait for what the night would hold, and I didn't want to suffer alone. Reaching for a napkin on the other side of Shane, I made sure my breasts pressed into him arm, enjoying the way the muscles tensed under me. When I pulled back, I met his eyes alit with fire.

"Sorry, I just needed a napkin real quick," I said with doe-eyed innocence.

"Careful."

I just smirked at his warning.

When he got his drink, he turned his body to face the rest of the group on the other side of me. An overly drunk patron pushed in front of me to get to the bar, shoving me back. I was irritated until, I found myself pressed close to Shane's front.

With everyone focused on a story Reese was sharing, I slipped my arm behind me, dragging my hand down until, I felt Shane's dick under my palm. He grunted and jerked, but the bar area was cramped and he had nowhere to pull back. I squeezed and rubbed, loving the way he slowly grew in my hand.

"Juliana," he growled behind me.

The drunk patron finally moved out of the way, giving me room to move. With one last stroke, I took a step forward, and grabbed my drink, needing the cool liquid to chill the heat trying to consume my body.

"Shane, we're going to play a round of darts," Reese called, motioning for Shane to follow them to the back.

"Um . . . Just a minute. Let me finish my beer."

I chuckled, knowing why he needed a minute. Couldn't walk away with a bulge tenting his pants. The guys moved to the back, and Shane took a full minute to down the rest of his drink. Before leaving, he turned to me.

"You're going to pay for that later, little girl."

"God, I hope so."

He ground his jaw and left to play darts. I spent the rest of the night dancing with the girls, imagining the best ways the night was going to go. All the positions, all the touching, everything.

When the party came to the end, thankfully everyone left at once, so it wasn't obvious when Shane and I walked out the door together. I wanted to follow him to his car and maybe give him road head, but that would have raised some red flags. Plus, I had to explain to Jolene that Shane was coming over.

"You may need to wear some headphones tonight," I said from the front seat of her car as she pulled out of the lot.

"Why?" She glanced over at me, looking confused.

"Shane is coming over."

"Aw, yeah! Get it girl!" She threw one hand up and let out a loud, "Ow-Ow!"

I laughed. "Stop."

She shrugged. "Can't promise I won't listen in."

"Ew."

"I'm just kidding . . . Kind of."

When we parked the car, I glanced at my reflection in the mirror, making sure none of my makeup was running, before meeting Shane at the elevators. He stood quietly as we rose, only giving a stiff smile to Jo.

She walked into the apartment and grabbed her headphones off the coffee table, making a big show of holding them up as she walked backward toward her room. "I'm going to be in my room all night. With my music up waaaay loud. Won't be able to hear a thing."

She gave me a quick wink and a gun before rounding the corner, followed by the slam of her door.

I looked back at Shane, who looked about as comfortable as a mouse trapped in the cage with a snake. "It's, uh, been a while since I've had to deal with a roommate. Probably since my twenties."

His comments about my age didn't usually bother me, but sometimes they stood out in a way that screamed how young I was. I couldn't help but imagine him seeing me like a child, and it pushed a button for me.

Pushing the feeling aside, I took a deep breath and remembered the excitement from before, determined to make him forget anyone but me. We were finally doing this and I was taking full advantage.

Grabbing his large hands in mine, I walked him to my room. He glanced around quickly, always observant. However, after locking the door, I walked around him, letting my nails drag across his chest and his attention focused only on me. Reaching up, I brushed his jacket off his shoulders and let it fall to the floor with a thud.

Slowly, I dropped to my knees kissing everything on my way down, letting my teeth drag along the growing thickness under his jeans before I scooted back and sat on the edge of the bed. Resting my hands on the mattress behind me, I arched my back, showcasing my breasts, and spread my legs.

He looked me up and down, his nostrils flaring in excitement. I watched his hand stroke himself through his pants, and I had to squeeze my core against the heat building there.

"You ever watch, little girl?"

My eyes flicked to him, widening at the possibilities of what he meant. "Like, porn?"

He chuckled at my suggestion. "No. Ever watched a man stroke himself until he came as he stared at your body? Ever watch *yourself* being taken?"

My mouth lacked all moisture and I swallowed hard, shaking my head.

His small chuckle and smirk excited me and scared me. *What was he going to have me do?*

He began unbuckling his belt, my eyes glued to the action. "Get naked, Juliana. Then slide back against the headboard."

Nodding my head, I began to strip, fumbling like a fool because my eyes were glued to each patch of newly exposed skin as he stripped before me. The way his abs and chest rippled as he pulled his shirt off. The way his thighs flexed when he toed off his shoes. All of it like my own personal strip show.

By the time I fumbled with the clasp on my bra he stood before me completely nude, proud. I slid my lace thong down my thighs and scooted back as instructed. He crawled up the bed, dragging his hands up from my ankles, past my knees, and down my inner thighs, spreading me wide. A hum rumbled in his chest as he stared at me and his hands gripped tightly against my thighs, pushing them further apart, exposing every part of me to his gaze.

Then he took my hand and moved it to my core. "Show me how you pleasure yourself. Show me how you played with yourself thinking of our night in Jamaica. Because I know you did. Let me watch you. And you watch me."

My cheeks burned, but with excitement. I wanted to be a brave woman for him, bold in my actions. Confident. I rolled my fingers around my clit, pulling wetness from my core up to glide across the bundle of nerves. My eyes wanted to fall shut and focus on the pleasure, but he told me to watch him and I didn't want to miss a second.

"First, I need some lube."

I was about to turn to reach in my bedside drawer when two thick fingers pushed in to me, curling on their way out. Then three, repeating the same motion. He would pull out and grip his cock, massaging my wetness along his length before going back for more.

His bicep bulged, stroking slowly from root to tip. His grip was harder than I would have ever tried and I became intrigued with the way the head of his cock would expand between his grip at the end of each stroke. I loved watching his lids get heavier and his eyes darken. He stared at every part of my body, but kept coming back to my exposed cunt. It squeezed in emptiness every time his fingers left me. His breathing picked up in pace along with his hand.

My hips undulated, getting closer and closer to release. I didn't want to come yet, so I made wider circles around my clit, making it last.

He started to groan and I was ready to watch the long white ropey cum shoot all over me, but his other hand came up and he squeezed his balls in one palm as the other created a tight circle around his cock.

"What are you doing?" I breathed the question, unable to speak past my panting breaths.

"I'm gonna fuck you, Mini MacCabe. But first I'm going to make you come. A few times."

"But I want to watch you come on me."

"Fuck," he growled the words. "I promise I will be sure to come on you later. But first I need to eat you out."

He dropped forward and wedged his shoulders between my thighs. I wanted to be upset for missing the show, but it was impossible when he'd pushed three fingers inside me and began flicking my clit frantically with his tongue. This wasn't a long drawn out orgasm, this was a freight train barreling down on me at record speed.

I screamed out my release and my whole body clenched around him, my thighs trembling from the effort of being spread. When I'd finally finished coming, I begged for Shane to stop as he continued to lap at my clit. He kissed his way up my body and slipped his tongue into my mouth, making me taste myself, before rolling to the side of me.

"Aren't you going to come?"

He laughed at my question. "Oh, I will Mini MacCabe. We aren't close to done yet."

My body didn't know how to feel about that as my pussy spasmed again and my legs still trembled from the strain.

But my heart beat hard and pumped heat through my veins. Yeah, I was ready for round two.

Shane got up, pulling me out of bed with him and supported me when my legs almost crumpled. He held me close as he led me to the corner of my bed and he sat. I stood lamely, waiting for instructions. When he pulled me to sit on his lap, I was met with our naked bodies reflected in the full-length mirror in front of me. My initial urge was to cover myself, but Shane held my arms down at my sides and leaned me back against him, my head falling against his shoulder.

"Do you know what I thought of when you sent me those pictures of you standing in front of this mirror in that sinful lingerie?" he asked against my ear.

I shook my head back and forth on his shoulder. "No."

He dragged his fingers down my thighs and gripped the inside of my knees. "I imagined bending you over and fucking you from behind in front of it, watching your tits bounce each time I shoved myself inside you."

"Do it," I whimpered.

"I will. But not yet." He shoved my knees apart to the outside of his spread legs, exposing me. His right hand moved up to my core and began slowly circling my opening. I clenched from being sensitive from my last orgasm. "First, I'm going to have you see what I see when I finger this tight little cunt. I'm going to let you watch the way your pert breasts heave on each heavy breath when you're on the verge of coming. The way your nipples pebble in excitement and make me want to bite them."

I moaned when he pushed two fingers inside me. Slowly, he dragged them back out and leisurely pushed back in.

"Look at you, Juliana. Look."

I tipped my head up and watched his long fingers disappear inside me. I watched the way they reappeared wetter than before when he pulled out. The way they rose to circle my clit before falling back down to push inside again. No rush, just enjoying the feel of my body inside and out.

"So fucking wet. Getting wetter when you stopped to watch. Do you like it? Does it make this little pussy ache with need, ache for a thick cock to fuck it when you get to see how beautiful it is taking my fingers?"

Beyond words, I could only moan. I was incapable of more than emitting groans gasps to express my pleasure.

He pulled out and lifted his hand to pinch at my nipples. He adjusted himself and his cock rose hard between my legs.

"Do you want to see the way this pretty pussy—*my* pretty pussy—stretches when I enter you? When I put myself inside your body?"

"Yes. Shane. Please."

He produced a condom like magic and slowly slid it on, like he was in no hurry, while my body shook with the urge to feel him inside me. To see it.

He lifted me and gripped his cock to line up with my opening. The tip just rested inside, barely, and he used both hands to hold my waist so he could control the speed at which he entered me.

I wanted to slam down over and over again, ride him like my own personal fuck toy. But he held me steady as inch by inch of him disappeared inside my vagina.

"Look at the way it stretches, accommodating me. Look at the way my dick comes out covered in your cum, your pussy so wet, so desperate for more."

He lowered me down a little harder the next time, groaning as he settled inside me. His pace grew faster and I watched him, watched us. My eyes frantic to take it all in. The way he looked pushing in and out of me, the desire burning across his face as he watched me, the way my tits bounced as he fucked me harder.

As we lost our rhythm and my orgasm began burning inside of me all over again, he wrapped an arm around my waist and stood, toppling us to the ground. I fell on all fours and he situated himself inside again, done with all pretense of going slow.

He gripped both my hips and pounded into me like an animal. One hand slid up my back into my hair and pulled, lifting me off my hands and into him.

"Look at those prefect breasts bounce with each thrust. Look at the way you make me lose control. Look at the way that perfect pussy takes me in."

I did. I took it all in and when he pinched my nipple and shoved in deep, coming inside me, I came. It poured over me in endless waves, his groans of pleasure the only thing keeping me in touch with reality.

He gently released me to the ground, but still thrust slowly a few more times until he had to pull out and remove the condom. He didn't even bother getting up to dispose of it, just tied it up and dropped it to the side, probably ruining something. I didn't care. He lay beside me and pulled me into his arms right there on the floor of my bedroom in front of my mirror.

I'd never be able to look in the mirror again the same way.

"Told you I was going to fuck you in the mirror."

He kissed my shoulder and somewhere in the ten minutes we tried to regain our strength, we fell asleep. I woke to him lifting me off the floor and putting me on my bed, where we started all over again.

Chapter Fifteen

"Feed meeee." I dragged the words out on a whine as I rolled over in bed, tugging the sheet to cover my naked breasts.

"I just did." He tugged the sheet back down to stare at my chest.

"Your dick is not enough to fill me up."

He cocked his head to the side and raised an eyebrow calling bullshit.

"That's not what I meant." I laughed and shoved his shoulder. "I need real food. Carbs. Meat. Fat."

"I don't think I have anything to eat here. I haven't ordered my groceries yet. Let me look through my menus." He began rolling out of bed, but I latched onto his arm.

"Ooo, what about that sushi place on the corner?"

"No, I got sick the last time I ate there. What about Mexican?"

"No, I had Mexican two nights ago and then leftovers last night."

It had been two weeks since we'd begun our adventure of sleeping together. We hadn't gone anywhere together other than to each other's apartments where we stayed to fuck and eat. My schedule revolved around how much of Shane's body I could get, which usually meant I wasn't home to make dinner. And unless Shane happened to cook for me, I had takeout. I was so sick of takeout.

"Okay . . ." He rubbed his hand over his hair. "I think I may have some crackers and cheese here."

"Really? Crackers and cheese? I will waste away here and not have enough energy to continue having sex. I need food."

"What if we run into someone while we're out?"

"Oh, my god." I flopped back on the bed and threw my arms wide in frustration. "Shane, Cincinnati is big. There is a slim to none chance that we will run into someone who would tell Jack." Rolling to my stomach, I held my hands together in prayer, giving my best puppy dog eyes. "I'm tired of ordering in. Let's go somewhere we can sit down. I promise to not expect a marriage proposal afterward. Feed. Me."

Laughing at my desperate plea, he still hesitated. "Okay."

I threw my arms up. "Yessss. I will not die of hunger this Friday night."

He just shook his head and rose from the bed, pulling on his boxer briefs. "You coming, Mini MacCabe?" he asked from the bathroom door.

I looked him up and down. His body always made my mouth water. "Not right now I'm not." I teased him.

"Don't worry. You will be later. But princess wants to be fed now. Get dressed and maybe I'll have you for dessert after dinner."

I squeezed my thighs in anticipation.

"Shane. This place has candied bacon. Candied bacon!" I practically bounced in my seat, I was so excited about the food.

"I told you you'd like this place."

"I'm so excited. And hungry."

"Obviously. I think you ordered enough to feed a small army."

"It's going to be fantastic. We can share the sides."

"All eight of them."

I grinned. People probably assumed I didn't eat much because I was thin, but I was just blessed with a fast metabolism and a lot of height to distribute my weight. I didn't eat horribly, but I didn't hold back at new places or on sweet glorious food in cast iron skillets.

Once I'd settled down, I rested my hands on the table and looked at my dinner companion. The low lighting of the bar cast a shadow along his face, highlighting the bruise along his cheekbone.

"So, you working a big case?"

He'd been busy lately and we'd had to squeeze in late night romps. I'd wake up with his arms wrapped around me, and take in his calm face in sleep. He always managed to surprise me when I woke up to him still there. Or when he wrapped me in his arms after thoroughly wearing me out at his place, expecting me to stay. I was always sure he would leave in the middle of the night like he'd done in Jamaica, or ask me to leave once we'd finished.

Only one time was I brave enough to ask why he didn't kick me out, and his brows had furrowed, as though he was just as confused as me, like he hadn't even realized it was happening. I held my breath waiting for his answer, fully expecting him to shrug, tell me I had a good point, and show me to the door. Instead, he'd smiled and said he enjoyed the possibility of morning sex.

That moment of hesitation and fear of disrupting our current situation prevented me from asking again.

"You know I can't talk about it."

"Come on. Jack shares stories about some of his cases."

"Yeah, when it has to do with a simple P.I. case and his employees somehow end up in a brothel."

I chuckled, remembering that story at last Sunday's brunch. "Can you at least confirm that the case caused the bruise on your cheek and the scrapes on your back?"

"Some people don't like to be questioned willingly."

My imagination took off thinking of big, bad, detective Shane chasing down a perp and his muscles strained as he took him to the ground and handcuffed him. Mmmmm . . .Handcuffs.

"I don't find you being a brave cop at all sexy."

"Trust me, it's not that sexy. Most people—women—get irritated by the hours. A lot of the men I work with who have families struggle every day to make their families a priority. The department takes its toll on a family. It's stressful and dangerous. They give me enough reason to never want to bring a family into that. I can focus on my job without anyone else to consider."

I fought to swallow the lump that had settled in my throat at his speech, trying not to hear it as a warning. I knew Shane didn't do serious, but over the past month, I've had to remind myself of that more and more when my heart skipped a beat at seeing him across a room.

"Jeez, Shane. Let me know how you really feel. I was just hoping to be arrested later and have you strip out of your uniform for me." I tried to break the tension his words had created by being funny.

He smirked at me and leaned in. "Maybe we can play cops and robbers later."

"Will you use your handcuffs?"

He growled under his breath just as our waitress settled the cornbread skillet on our table. I hummed as I took each bite, loving the sweet warm bread on my tongue. Shane watched with a smile, sometimes laughing at my excitement. Like when I clapped as our meal was set on the table. It all barely fit on the small square for two.

A quarter of a chicken for me, and a half for him, and of course the candied bacon, French fries, mac and cheese, coleslaw, mashed potatoes, succotash, and sweet potatoes with toasted marshmallows on top.

I started digging in as soon as the waitress walked away. I didn't even ask if he minded me dipping my spoon into his cast iron side dishes, I just went for it. He took my cue and did the same. I dipped my French fry in the aioli and moaned with the first bite.

With my mouth full and another French fry in hand, I pointed at the aioli. "You have to try that. I usually love ketchup, like truly love ketchup, but that aioli is the jam."

He laughed, but followed orders, nodding his head at my review. "I had a foster brother who loved ketchup. Used to drink it with a straw."

"Ew. I love ketchup, but that is taking it too far."

"He was definitely an odd one."

"Jack's right there with him. He used to mix his ketchup with mayo, and dredge his fries in it."

"Yeah, I've seen him do that before."

I licked a scoop of sweet potatoes off my spoon and swallowed, broaching a new subject he didn't talk about much. "You keep in touch with your foster brother?"

"No. He was only seven and I was out of there within the year."

"Why?" I didn't have a very good understanding of the foster system.

"I was given back to my mom after she proved she was clean."

"That's good."

He laughed without humor, and dragged his spoon through the mashed potatoes, making a swirling patter. "Not really. I was with her less than a year before she got caught with drugs again and they pulled me. That was the last time I saw her."

"She never got clean again?" I pushed to keep a blank face, because even though he wasn't looking at me, I didn't want him to look up and think he saw pity there. Shane was not a man to be pitied.

"No. She died of an overdose, and I was in the system from there on out."

I didn't apologize. He wouldn't have wanted it. "Did you stay with any one family for long?"

"Probably the longest I stayed with one, was for two years." Deep ridges formed between his eyebrows and his throat worked up and down before he shook his head and continued. "I'd already been with a couple of families before then. Moved around a lot. I wasn't exactly an easy kid. Not horrible, but not easy."

"I think that still applies to you," I said, trying to keep it light.

When I chuckled, he looked up at me for the first time since he started talking about his childhood. He looked relieved and grateful that I didn't baby him and laughed too.

"Seems to work for you," he accused.

"I guess it does. I'll get shirts made. *Looking for a man that isn't horrible, but not easy either.*"

"You can add it to your collection of shirts."

We laughed through dinner as I over-ate. Our waitress brought the check around and Shane paid.

"You didn't have to do that. I think I ate more than you."

"I think you did too, but it's not a big deal."

He stood in front of me as I put on my jacket, doing his regular cop thing checking out the bar.

"Fuck. *Fuck.*"

"What?" I looked up into his wide eyes staring beyond my shoulder and began looking around too. He grabbed my arm and tugged me toward the back of the restaurant. "Shane. What the hell?"

He ducked down a hallway and looked side to side at the doors. "Your brother and Lu were sitting about five booths away. They were heading in our direction. Thank god I spotted him before he saw me."

He pushed open the first door that didn't lead to the kitchen and looked side to side before yanking me into the women's restroom.

"What the hell? What if someone comes in?"

"This never would've happened if you just would've been happy with Mexican food."

"Oh, well, I'm sorry for wanting to eat something a little bit more than food from a box. This is not my fault," I said in a hard voice.

He ignored me. "You brother can't see us together."

"Why?" I got it, I did. Shane didn't want to shout from the rooftops that we were fucking, especially to my brother since Jack would lose his shit. But it wouldn't be the end of the world if we were caught having dinner together. It's not like he would see Shane and I going at it.

"Your brother is my best friend—my family, and he would murder me if he knew I was hanging out with you." He ran a hand through his hair as he paced.

"I'm an adult, Shane." I enunciated each word, letting him know how irritated I was at his irrationality. The whole family thing was making more sense after what he'd just shared, but it didn't give him a pass to drag me around and hide me like a dirty secret. "My brother-"

The sound of voices from the hallway grew louder as they neared the ladies room, halting the beginning of my tirade. My eyes widened in his direction. He pushed a stall door open and pulled me in. Thankfully they were full length doors so no one could see underneath.

The bathroom door creaked and Lu said, "Cleaning. Anyone in here?"

Shane held his finger to his lip. I was more worried they'd be able to hear my angry-mixed-with-panicked breathing.

"It's all clear, come on," Lu whispered.

Then there was the worst sound of my entire life. Wet, sucking faces noises. Moans. My brother's fucking moans. Then came the rustling of clothes and sweet god almighty I would *not* sit there and listen to them fuck.

I gave Shane a warning look, and I wanted to slap the amused look right off of his face. He was trying to hide it, but doing a poor job. I shook my head, and he held his finger up to my lips, mouthing, *Wait*.

I shuddered at Lu's giggles.

"Remember the last time I fucked you in a public bathroom. I love how excited you got. Your pussy so tight."

My jaw dropped, on the brink of unhinging completely from my face. Shane had to hold a hand over his mouth to hold back his laughter. I didn't know if he was enjoying the show outside or my sheer disgust.

"God, you're so wet."

I threw up in my mouth a little. Or at least made the motion of almost throwing up. And Shane broke, letting out the smallest laugh. But it was enough to alert our presence.

"Fuck," Lu said. "Someone's in here." Clothes rustled back in place and Shane gestured at me to say something. Like I was going to step out with jazz hands, making sure they knew the horrible last five minutes were going to haunt me forever.

Instead, I settled on an odd, Irish-Spanish, high pitched accent. "So, sorry. Didn't want to ruin your good time."

Shane's chest vibrated with laughter, and I pinched his nipple, making him jerk.

"Shit. Sorry," Jack apologized. "Just a little horny. But getting out of here now. Sorry. So sorry."

The door opened and closed announcing their exit, and Shane had to rest a hand on the wall to hold himself up, he was laughing so hard.

"Not. Fucking. Funny." I said each word with a smack to his body, but he didn't stop. The humor surrounding the horrid situation broke the tension from earlier and I began to smile and hold back my own laughter. "Keep it up and you won't get dessert," I warned with a straight face, reminding him of his promise from earlier.

He pulled himself together, barely. "We'll see."

And we did.

We snuck out the back and once we made it to the car, he pulled me into the backseat and ate me out—getting his dessert.

Chapter Sixteen

"You're my tour guide today." I spread my arms out to the side when Shane opened the door to my announcement.

"What?"

"We're going out."

He cocked an eyebrow at me and pursed his lips. "Do I need to remind you about the last time we went out?"

"Yeah. You went down on me in the back seat of your car and it was awesome."

"We also listened to your brother talk dirty to his wife."

"Unimportant." I waved his comment away refusing to ever think of it again.

"Shane, Cincinnati is so big," he said high-pitched, mocking my words from the last time I'd convinced him to go out with me. "There is a slim-to-none chance anyone will see us."

I gave him a deadpanned stare.

"One, I am not amused by your imitation." Then I reached in

my oversized purse and pulled out a hat and sunglasses. "And two, I thought ahead. Look, I got us disguises."

I slipped them on and waggled my eyebrows at him. When he opened his mouth to talk, I held up my hand, signaling him to wait. I dug in my pocket and pulled out a sticky felt mustache and stuck it on my upper lip.

"You've already got that hot as hell five o'clock shadow going on, but they'll never recognize me with my sweet mustache."

Finally, he laughed, shaking his head at my absurdity.

"If anyone sees us, we'll say we just happened to run into each other. No one will suspect anything. Come on," I whined. "I've lived here almost a year and haven't explored any hidden gems. I did all my homework this week for the lab, and we're both free this weekend. It's gorgeous outside and Google and I created a sweet ass itinerary for today. Show me your city you love so much."

"How do you know I love it so much?"

"All the pictures hanging in your apartment for one. And you live to protect it. Duh. You kind of have to love the city to risk your life for it."

He chuckled, like he was surprised I noticed all that. "I guess you're right."

"Of course, I'm right. Now grab your stuff and let's go."

"Fine. But if we run into anyone, I'm going to pretend to not be into you and probably bail. You don't get to be pissed about that."

I couldn't help but be a little annoyed, but I understood his stance, so I held up my hands in surrender. "I solemnly swear to not be mad, as long as I can meet you back here and you make it up to me with your mouth."

He laughed. "One more thing . . .you need to take that damn mustache off."

"Fine." I rolled my eyes and peeled it off before shoving it in my purse. When he turned to me after locking his door, I waggled my eyebrows again. "I'll save it for later tonight."

His laugh followed me down the stairs as we headed to his car. First stop of the day was Findlay Market. I'd looked it up online and was instantly excited by all the options and colors.

However, once we parked and strolled up to the crowds of people with the early spring sun shining down on us, the pictures online couldn't compare. I grabbed Shane's hand when we braved the crowds, weaving in and out of the red tables filled with people, not wanting to lose him.

"Do you want to go inside, or stroll the tents on either side?" he asked, his shoulders tense as he scanned the crowd, looking for anyone who may know us.

"I don't know. Whatever you think is best. I'm so overwhelmed in the best way. There's everything here."

"Yeah, Findlay Market is kind of like Seattle's Pike Place."

"I've never been there either, but I've heard of it."

"Let's start inside and work our way out. It's still a little chilly this morning."

As we made our way from shop to shop, Shane's shoulders slowly relaxed, and he began to stop looking everywhere, turning his attention all on me. It was intoxicating.

We'd hold hands when we needed to make it through a crowd, but as the day wore on, he stopped dropping my hand when we got to an opening. I wasn't even sure he realized he was doing it. I thought about saying something, making a joke, but I didn't want to do anything to make it stop. Instead, I held tight and enjoyed the feeling while it lasted.

We walked past food vendors and tasted meats and fruits and whatever samples they had out, each flavor somehow better than the last.

Shane laughed when we made our way outside to a vendor tent and I oohed and aahed over the cards and mugs.

"I love the funny cards, the dirtier the better. Even if I don't have a reason to buy them, I'll get them anyway to look through later. Oh, and check out this mug." I pulled it from the rack and held it up to him. *I'd love to stay and chat but I'm lying.*

He laughed and pulled it from my hands, taking it to the check out. "We'll take this one."

"You don't have to do that."

"I know. I want to. I noticed all your mugs in the kitchen. Pretty interesting for someone who doesn't drink hot coffee."

"It doesn't have to be coffee to use it. It's still just a cup. Besides, I love hot chocolate."

"Fair enough." He took his change and reached for my hand as we walked out.

Next on our list was Shane's choice. I'd found a small local restaurant, but he'd vetoed it and said I hadn't lived until I'd had Larosa's.

I'd told him I'd never had it and he threw his hand to his chest and gasped like a true Southern belle, claiming we couldn't do anything else until he shared the glory of Cincinnati pizza.

I couldn't deny how right he was. When we walked in, the smell alone was almost orgasmic. His jaw clenched when I'd moaned as the waiter set the pizza in front of us. We got a classic cheese and a meat deluxe.

I pulled the cheese off the top and began eating it.

"What the hell are you doing?"

"Eating, why?"

"Why are you pulling the cheese off?"

"Because I like to enjoy each part individually. This pizza is kind of awesome because when I pull off the cheese, all the toppings are underneath. Like little surprises." He stared at me like I'd grown a unicorn head on my shoulder. I gave him a big smile and popped the cheese in my mouth, moaning at the flavor.

"You're weird as hell."

"You love it," I said with a mouth full of bacon, sausage, and pepperoni. "What other food does Cincinnati have? Can we try something else tonight?"

"Don't worry, Mini MacCabe. I'll introduce you to all the foods Cincinnati has to offer. Sometime soon, I'll have to take you to Skyline Chili."

"Ooo, I've had that. Jolene and I stumbled upon it one day. It's delicious. It's not really chili. More of a crumble of meat in some sauce, but I loved it."

We paid our bill and it was already closing in on three in the afternoon. We had one more stop that I'd looked up: Eden Park.

We strolled hand in hand along the beautiful walking path, the trees just beginning to bloom. He explained the different architecture like the Eden Park Standpipe and the Elsinore Arch. It was all so gorgeous. There was also entirely too much to do before it got dark.

"We'll come back and do the conservatory and art museum another day."

"Promise?"

"I promise."

With his word locked in place, I followed him back to the car.

"Well, that's all I had planned for the day."

"Let me take you to one more food place. It's on Fountain Square."

"Oh, I've never been. Driven past about four thousand times, but I've never stopped to walk around."

"There's a really good ice cream place there."

I clapped my hands I was so excited. I loved ice cream.

He parked in the garage and led the way to a place called Grater's. I walked in, looked at all the handmade ice cream, and my eyes lit up. There were so many flavors, I couldn't decide.

"What do you want?" he asked.

"All of it."

He laughed. "As much as I would love to see you eat it all, I don't want you to be sick later tonight." He smirked and I nudged him with my shoulder, laughing at his meaning.

"Okay. You pick for me."

"Hmmm. How about we stay with the theme of Cincinnati and go with the Buckeye Chocolate Chip."

"Sounds glorious."

And it was. We ate our ice cream and people watched from our table next to the window. When I'd practically licked my paper cup clean, we went to walk around the Square.

We stood in front of the huge fountain, the lights shining all over it, as water poured from the top, flowing over the many layers. I shivered as we looked up at the top and he pulled me into his arms, holding my back tight to his front. He kept me warm with more than just his arms. He made me feel special, cared for, and safe, and I wanted to stay there forever. I wanted to kiss him.

I maneuvered around in his arms, to face him and smiled up at him. "Thank you for today."

"Thank you. It's been a while since I've toured my own city."

He leaned down at the same time I lifted my chin and pressed my lips to his. They were cold from the ice cream and the chill outside since night settled. The kiss was slow, like we were trying to memorize every detail of the other's lips. When his tongue brushed along the seam of my lips, I opened, letting him taste me. We didn't rush, just let our hands slide up and down each other's backs and made out like a couple of teenagers in public.

When we heard salsa music coming from the other side of the fountain, we pulled back, and I stepped away to see what it was.

"They're teaching salsa." I looked back at him with wide eyes, excitement pouring off me.

"Juliana," he warned.

"Come on," I pleaded. "There's an instructor and everything. We can hide in the back."

He held firm until I started swirling my hips and backing away toward the crowd. He begrudgingly followed, and a huge grin split my face at his acceptance.

We stood in the back and tried to move our hips the way the teacher showed. The instructor would come around and help us find the rhythm and correct our foot placement. Every time I looked over at Shane, he seemed to be doing his own thing, struggling to find the rhythm. I tried not to laugh, but he stiffened every time the teacher tried to help him move his hips. He'd glare at me, and I'd just twirl in a circle, swiveling my hips for him.

Soon everyone was set free to practice their newly learned moves on their own on the dance floor as the band played songs. The instructors did the dance in the middle so people could follow if they wanted, but I decided to swirl my hips and dance circles around Shane.

I noticed some people stopping and staring at my excitement and the show I put on for Shane, but it didn't bother me. All I needed were his blazing eyes scorching over me as I shook my ass at him. All I needed was the feel of his muscles clenching under my hand as I dragged it across his back and chest.

The song ended and Shane stepped into me, leaning down to my ear. "I'm ready to go." His words were spoken barely above a whispered growl, the air brushing against the sensitive skin of my neck. I nodded and let him take my hand in his and lead the way.

We had to cross the street to get back to our garage and when we stood at the corner, waiting for the light, I could still hear the music and decided to dance against him. The people on the crowded corner probably thought I was a drunk. But I didn't care.

I lived for the twitch of his lips that formed a small smile as he watched me. I closed my eyes and moved my shoulders to the beat, and when I opened them and looked up at him, his smile was gone. His brows furrowed and he looked at me as though he'd never seen me before. The intensity of how hard he stared hammered at my chest, but I didn't know what he was thinking when he took me in.

"What?" I asked quietly, not even sure he heard me.

He closed his eyes and shook his head before letting another smile stretch across his face. "Nothing."

The light turned green and we ran across the street. I laughed, dancing around him until the salsa music faded in the background. Throughout our walk, he continued to stare at me the same way as he had on that corner. His bright eyes blazing hot along my skin. They looked me over as though trying to find something he hadn't noticed before. My chest felt tight and hot, and I wanted to dance for him forever if it meant he never stopped watching me the way he was. I was forced to stop swaying around him when he snagged my arm and pulled me in for a deep kiss.

He held me tightly to him like I'd slip away. He didn't stop to breathe, but breathed through his nose, taking me in, brushing his tongue against mine. I clung to his shirt, feeling the heat, the passion, the desperation behind his kiss.

A horn honking and a man yelling for us to get a room separated us. I pulled back with a giddy smile and kissed his nose.

"That's a good idea. Take me home, Shane."

Chapter Seventeen

We stayed silent in the car while Shane held my hand the whole time, stealing glances in my direction.

We stayed silent when he parked the car and entered my apartment building.

We stayed silent in the elevator ride up to my floor.

We stayed silent as I unlocked my door and his hands roamed my body from breasts to hips, his lips kissing from my shoulder up to my ear.

The silence greeted us when I opened my apartment. The darkness letting me know Jolene wasn't home.

It was the last silence of the night until our moans, grunts, and pleas would become the only thing to echo within the walls.

I dropped my purse and he kicked the door shut behind us and pulled me into him, my back to his front. His hands started at my stomach and rose up to cup my breasts as his mouth made love to my neck. Tipping my head to the side, I moaned and chills raced down my spine, tingling out to my limbs, my skin rising in goose bumps to reach him.

I pushed my hips back into his groin and placed my hand over his, moving it down to between my legs. He gripped me hard there and growled one word.

"Mine."

I was. In his arms, in that moment, I was his.

He flipped me around and hoisted me up, bringing my legs to wrap around his waist. We held each other's stare as he walked us to my room. His ice blue eyes heating and darkening, his pupils dilating, and the anticipation of what they promised burned through me.

I expected frantic. I expected to be tossed on the bed and clothes to be torn off. Instead, he gently lay me down, locking his lips on mine and grinding against me as we melded our tongues and our bodies together. Still fully clothed, we let our hands roam and panted against each other, gasping for breath between each kiss.

"Please, Shane," I whispered against his lips, needing more. The throb between my legs becoming too much with not enough to satisfy it.

He leaned back and pushed my hands away when I went to tear off my shirt, stopping me from stripping, so he could do it for me. He revealed each piece of my skin like it was the last present he'd ever get to open and wanted to cherish it forever. He kissed each exposed body part gently, dipping his tongue into my belly button, swirling it around each of my breasts to only leave a soft sucking kiss to the nipples.

He leaned back and held my stare as he tugged his shirt over his head, his chest and abs rippling from the movement, before falling back on top of me, scalding my skin with his own. We felt like fire and heat, and I was dying to go up in flames with him. My hands roamed his chest, dragging them down, gently circling his nipples with my fingers before moving further to undo his belt.

He let me get as far as the zipper, and when I was about to reach my hand inside to feel him in the palm of my hand, he backed up, sliding down my body, leaving sucking kisses in his wake. He fell to his knees on the floor and dragged my pants and underwear from my body, kissing down my thighs, knees, and calves before finally slipping them off. Then he made his way back up again, parting my thighs, rubbing his thumbs up and down the lips of my pussy, taunting me with what was to come.

I lifted my hips, begging him without words to touch me, to lick me, to taste me. He placed sucking kisses along my groin and when I looked down to watch his mouth on me, my eyes locked with his. Holding my stare, he finally parted my lips and dragged his tongue from my opening to my clit. I cried out from the pleasure, my head falling back to the bed.

He repeated his ministrations, up and down, up and down. He'd spend time at my bundle of nerves and then he would plunge his tongue in and out of me, holding my thighs as far apart as they would go and then pushing them back to expose every inch of me.

I almost came off the bed when he slipped past my core and dropped lower to my rosette.

"Shane." I gasped, shocked and unsure of the feeling. He continued with flicks of his tongue, touching nerve endings I didn't even know existed. He moved one hand to my cunt and plunged two fingers in to my wetness. Slow, measured thrusts. When he removed them, he replaced them with his tongue, but then moved his fingers to my tight hole and began pushing a finger inside me.

Unintelligible whimpers escaped from my throat, unsure of the electricity firing through my body. His finger pushed harder, stretching me, and his tongue moved back to my clit, quickly flicking back and forth. It was too much. Too much pleasure and too many sensations consumed me, and I gasped for air, clinging to the sheets as a heat fell over me.

I cried out as my orgasm crashed over me in waves over and over again, his finger pushing in and out of my ass, his tongue a relentless movement around my core, not letting me come down from my high.

When I did come back, I had tears streaming down my temples and my chest heaved with choked sobs. It was too much, and my body didn't know how to handle it.

"Shh. Shh." Shane soothed me as the bed dipped and he laid over me, wiping the wet tracks from my face. "You did so well. So beautiful. I've never seen anything quite so extraordinary as you when you come."

His words wrapped around me, soothing the frantic pace of my heart. The way his eyes stared down at me made me feel an acceptance I'd never had before. It made my heart race and my eyes burn for a whole other reason. He looked at me like he adored me, like I was his only purpose in life.

I heard the crinkle of a condom wrapper before I felt the tip of his cock brushing against my opening. I clenched my core, even the slight brush of his tip against my swollen cunt sent a shock through my body.

He held my stare, brushing the hair back from my sweaty face, as he pushed in slowly, an inch at a time, not stopping until he was seated as deep as he could go, his balls resting against my ass.

He held my stare as he pulled out and repeated the process, swirling his hips, grinding into my clit each time he pushed in. His forehead rested against mine, our breaths mixing in the small space between us as he slowly fucked me.

No.

This wasn't fucking. This was beyond different than anything we'd shared before. There was no fast pace, no skin slapping against the other's, no dirty words stroking the flames higher. I hesitated to call it making love, but it felt like it, because I'd never felt anything so big before. It wrapped around us in our own little world. Him inside me, taking his time, relishing the mix of our heat.

"I wish I didn't need a condom," he whispered into my neck. "I wish I could feel you. Feel my cum deep inside you."

"I'm sorry." I didn't know what else to say. I was sorry, because I almost wanted to be crazy and risk everything to feel it. Even if I wasn't on birth control. "I'll get on birth control. I want to feel your cum inside me."

My words caused the first interruption in his pace. His hips jerking a little harder at the image my words must have painted.

He licked the beads of sweat up my neck as I clung to his back, lifting my legs higher on his hips, needing more of him. Needing all of him.

His hand reached down to grip my thigh, pushing up and over his shoulder and pushed hard into me, bringing a cry from my lips.

Watching my mouth, he did it again. And again. The thrusts coming faster and harder. I was so close, my cries becoming constant moans of rising pleasure as I chased my second orgasm of the night. He'd dragged out the time he was inside me, making it seem endless and now we both needed to come.

"Yes. Shane. Please."

He brought his lips to mine and began thrusting into me hard, grinding on my clit with each pass, until I couldn't take it anymore and my pussy began to spasm hard, spreading through my whole body, harder and faster than the last. He moaned against my lips, holding himself inside me as my cunt milked an orgasm from his cock.

When we were done, he slipped out of me and fell to the side, bringing me with him still in his arms. Our chests heaved from the exertion, and I dragged my hand across the sweat along his chest, wanting to remember this night forever. Needing to remember it.

Because that night, I fell in love with Shane.

Chapter Eighteen

The next morning, I rolled over and stretched my arms across the bed, expecting to find Shane.

Instead, cold sheets rested under my palm. Déjà vu hit me, the same feeling I'd had in Jamaica when I'd woken up to him gone. The disappointment pinching my chest. The hope that he'd come strolling back in and want more of me. But as I listened for sounds from my bathroom or the kitchen, I knew he'd left.

I rose to my elbows and looked around the room for his pants, shoes, anything, still imagining he was there despite the silence. All I found was a small piece of paper resting on his pillow.

I had to work this morning.
Shane

That was it. No apology, no regret, no nothing. Worse, was I knew he hadn't had to work today. We'd talked about how he'd had the weekend off and made jokes about ways to spend the day.

My foolish mind had conjured images of waking up next to him and repeating last night. My mind screamed at me to not push, but my heart pumped harder and harder, urging me to tell Shane what he meant to me.

In the end, my mind won out and I pushed the doubts about why he'd left down, telling myself that he got a call and something came up at the station.

I grabbed my phone from my nightstand and pulled up my messages. I'd just ask what happened and give him a reason to hurry back to me.

Me: I missed you this morning. Did something come up at work?

Me: Hopefully it doesn't take too long. I'd really love to have you for dinner. Until then, here's something to tide you over.

I tugged the sheets so they barely covered my vagina and exposed my stomach and legs. Taking a picture, I sent it and waited for his reply.

I imagined him sending one in return and we'd go back and forth, building the anticipation of the night to come. I imagined him calling me and getting me off with his words alone. I imagined him telling me he hated leaving and couldn't wait to get back to me.

I imagined wrong.

He never responded.

As the night wore on, I became worried that something had gone wrong. Maybe he was hurt. I watched the news a little closer that night, listening for anything that might have had to do with Shane. At one point, I'd thought about calling Jack and asking if he'd heard from Shane, but I knew I couldn't.

Shane and I had two rules: no telling Jack and just sex.

I was breaking the just sex rule, but I couldn't help it. Not with the way he'd loved me last night. Not with the way he'd held my hand and danced with me. A stone wall would have crumbled under that kind of tenderness.

And a part of me felt like Shane's stone wall was crumbling too.

But when Monday rolled around with still no response, I doubted what I'd felt. Maybe I'd imagined the whole night. Maybe I'd inferred my feelings to him and saw what I wanted. Maybe I was wrong.

On my way home from work, I sent another message.

Me: Hope you're okay.

I typed up about ten more messages. *I love you. I miss you. Do you care for me? Don't you miss me?* I deleted all of them and had to hold off from sending another message when it was ten o'clock and I still hadn't heard from him.

I couldn't sleep, so I pulled out my research articles and began reading, needing something to take my mind off Shane. It wasn't until midnight that I heard a soft knock at the door.

My heart skipped a beat, excited that it could be Shane. But I tamped down the hope, because it could also be a serial killer. Knocks at the door in the middle of the night usually had one of two purposes. Sex or death.

Looking through the peep-hole, I realized I was probably going to get sex.

I took my time opening the door, trying to decide which emotion would win out. Anger that he'd blown me off. Excitement that he was here. Horny because I knew why he'd shown up at my door in the middle of the night.

"Well, look what the cat dragged in. Alive and with all his fingers." He cocked an eyebrow, stepping into the apartment. "I figured you'd probably lost them and that was why you didn't text me back."

He didn't respond as I shut the door behind him, and when I turned to demand an explanation, he swooped in. His lips crashed against mine as he lifted me off the ground, my legs automatically wrapping around him.

I knew I should have stopped until he'd apologized for ignoring me. But I couldn't help but become lost in his kiss, in the feel of his body under my hands, his muscles bunching as he hoisted me higher aligning my core along his erection.

Moaning into his mouth, I rocked my hips and kissed him. Tried to figure out where he'd been just from what his kiss tasted like. But all I was met with was fresh mint barely masking the flavor of beer on his tongue.

He slammed me against the door and dropped his lips down my neck, licking, biting, sucking. I dug my hands into his short hair and tugged him back to look into my eyes. The blue burned dark and desperate. I searched for the same emotions I saw the last time we were together, but the more I looked, the more guarded he seemed to become.

"Is Jo here?"

I nodded my head. And with a growl, he pushed us off the wall and stalked toward my bedroom. He tossed me on the bed and kicked the door shut behind him before falling to his knees and frantically tugging off my sleep shorts.

"Shane." I breathed out his name in pleasure, begging him to never stop and pleading that he do so we could talk.

But he ignored it and dragged me to the edge of the bed where he knelt on the floor. He wedged his shoulders between my spread thighs and dropped his head, dragging his tongue from my opening to my clit. It was the only soft drag that he gave before using his thumbs to spread me and devour my cunt.

His tongue was fast. His mouth sucking hard. His teeth nipping. When he shoved two fingers inside me, I came hard, bringing my hand to my mouth to mask the heavy moans I couldn't contain.

He stood, wiping his mouth with the back of his hand before he sucked his fingers cleaned. I didn't even get a chance to move back and gather myself before he'd unbuckled his pants, tugging them down just far enough to free his length and slide on a condom.

He moved to me and gripped the back of my thighs, raising them high to my chest, and lined up the head of his dick with my opening. His eyes flicked to mine as he began easing into me, flashing with heat and want and need. Flashing with the same emotions from last time. "Shane."

He looked away, back down to where just the tip of him was lodged inside me, and watched himself slip further and further until there was nothing else to give. He pulled out slowly, and I yelped when he roughly pumped himself back in, making my breasts bounce under my shirt.

Repeating the same slow, rough process again and again, his eyes never once left where we were joined. I needed him to look at me, to be there with *me*. Not just focused on the fucking, but seeing *me*.

I leaned up and gripped the back of his neck, pulling him down to me so I could kiss him. I pressed my lips to his, pleading for more. Dragging my tongue along the seam of his lips, demanding he let me in. On a groan, he opened and his tongue tangled with mine.

He lost his easy rhythm, and his hips moved faster as our kiss became more desperate for each other. Placing his full weight on me, he held me close and fucked me like we hadn't been together for a year, rather than just one night.

His hands roamed my body, cupping my breasts, brushing my nipples, touching all of me. The room echoed with the sound of our flesh coming together, with our moans as we got closer to coming.

I chanted his name and his hand dropped between us, stroking my clit, sending me over the edge.

Gripping his neck, I pressed my forehead to his and came, looking into his eyes. Letting him see what he did to me. Almost as soon as I came down from my high he began coming. His hips pushing hard into me, holding himself inside me, trying to get deeper than before.

I expected his eyes to close, for him to hide from me. Instead he held my stare as groan after groan escaped his lips. It was so intense and filled with so many emotions, I forgot everything but the way my heart stretched against my chest.

Leaning up, I brushed my lips with his and held him close to me, wanting to press all my love into him, needing him to know how much I cared.

He slipped out of me and pulled back to remove the condom. I smiled, expecting him to finish taking off his clothes and to climb into bed next to me. But a pinch of doubt hit me when, instead, I saw him tuck himself back into his pants and redo his buckle.

"What are you doing?" I asked, sitting up, trying to catch his eyes. But he wouldn't look at me.

"I have to go. I have to be back at the station early in the morning."

"Stay with me." I knew I sounded like I was begging, but I didn't want to lose him again for another two days. I wanted him to hold me and wake up to him in the morning.

He finally looked up and scanned my face. He took so long to answer, I was sure he'd give in. But his brows furrowed more and more and on a heavy swallow, before the words even left his lips, his head was shaking. "Not tonight, Juliana."

Thank god it was dark in my room because tears burned the backs of my eyes at his rejection.

"Yeah. Okay." I swallowed too, trying to move back the lump in my throat. "Maybe tomorrow."

But when he looked at me again, I knew the answer.

"Have a good night." And with a small smile, he walked out the door, leaving me half naked on the edge of my bed, confused about what the fuck had just happened.

When I went into the station the next day, I gave myself a pep-talk. He was just busy. It hadn't meant anything that he had to leave. Maybe he'd just needed to relieve some stress. I wanted to be there for him.

And I tried to remind myself of the look in his eyes when he came. I tried to remember the desperate way he'd held me like he needed me. I focused on that over the disappointment of him leaving.

But it was hard to keep that up when he barely acknowledged me at the station. We'd sat at lunch and he'd kept his head down most of the conversation and left before everyone else. I'd tried to catch up to him before I left the building to ask him over for dinner, but he was already gone.

I wanted to send a message, but I was too scared of the rejection again. If I didn't push, I wouldn't have to deal with it. And when I hadn't heard from him by twelve-thirty, I finally caved and went to bed.

I'd been staring at the ceiling, trying to make my mind relax enough to pass out when I heard the soft knock on the front door. I hopped out of bed and practically sprinted to open it, making sure to check it was him.

As soon as the door opened, he was on me. He didn't even ask if Jo was home. There was no foreplay, just desperation. He didn't even bother moving to my room that time.

He undid his pants and slipped on a condom before lifting me against the wall, pushing my panties aside and shoving inside me. I tried to be quiet, knowing Jo was sleeping just on the other side of the wall, but it was impossible.

He buried his head in my neck and said my name over and over as he pressed into me, quickly, roughly. With the pace he set, we came in no time at all. I was sure he was going to stay when he'd held himself inside me and pulled back to look into my eyes. He'd stroked my cheek and pressed a gentle kiss to my lips.

And then let me down, removed the condom, and began buckling up his pants again.

"Shane," I'd pleaded for him to stop. To look at me and explain.

His jaw clenched as he gave me the briefest of glances. "Work's just really busy right now." And then he was gone.

The next morning when I walked out to the kitchen, Jo sat with a mug in her hands, watching me.

"Where's Shane?" When I looked up, wondering how she knew, she explained. "I heard you again last night."

"Sorry." Jo had taken great pleasure in letting me know she'd heard us Monday night. "He had to go."

"Again?"

"Yeah. He said he's just busy with work."

"Jules . . .I didn't let her continue with where she was going with her soft tone. I had enough doubts. I didn't need hers too.

"It's fine."

But it became less and less fine each night he came to me and left as soon as we'd finished.

Chapter Nineteen

I woke to Shane's heavy arm wrapped around my waist, holding me tightly to him, and smiled. I was shocked that he'd stayed after leaving every night the past week. On Thursday, I'd offered to come to him, and he'd brushed it off saying he hadn't wanted me to be driving in the middle of the night just for him to have to leave before the sun rose.

I would've stayed awake all day and night just to hold his hand, to feel his lips press to mine just a little. Our night of making love, of more than just fucking, had woken something in me. I was no longer content to "just fuck." He made me laugh. He made me feel confident, worthy of a man's love because I was a strong woman. I never wanted to lose that.

So, when he would only come back to me during sex, when I saw that spark of more behind his eyes as he buried himself inside me, I took it. I grabbed on with both hands and fought to not let go. I had to have hope, because despite his crazy schedule, he came to me every night.

But he never stayed. At least, until this morning.

I didn't want to wake him, so I gently rolled out from under his arm and sat up, looking back over my shoulder to the sleeping giant beside me. Clenching my fists to stop from touching him, I stood, then put a shirt and shorts on and headed to make him coffee.

Jolene stood against the counter scrolling through her phone, having already started the coffeemaker.

"Morning," she said, not looking up.

"Morning." I reached into the cabinet and grabbed two mugs, setting them on the counter, waiting with her.

She finally looked over at me, taking in the two cups.

"*Two* mugs?"

"Yeah." I shrugged like it was no big deal and opened the fridge to start making my iced coffee mix. "Shane's asleep in the bedroom."

She mock-gasped and brought her hand to her chest. "What? No wham-bam-thank-you-ma'am?"

I gave her a strong disapproving side eye. "Stop it. He's just been busy at work."

Jolene had seen the difference in me since our one night. She'd also seen how I'd fallen throughout the week as he pulled away more and more.

"Whatever you say." She shrugged and began looking at her phone again. "I just don't want you to get hurt."

I didn't respond, because I wasn't sure I could guarantee that I wouldn't.

I poured the coffee and mixed one sugar in the way he liked it, grabbed my cup and entered to find Shane just waking up.

His muscles flexed and strained as he stretched his arms overhead, making my queen-size bed look like a toddler bed with his feet hanging over and his hands pressing against the head board.

"Morning." Once I was done with my ogling, I walked over and handed him a mug after he sat up.

"Ah." He took the mug and turned it in his hands, smiling at the saying. *Here's a cup of calm the fuck down.* "The famous mugs."

I rested my back against the headboard and twisted to face him. "I picked one just for you."

"Are you saying I'm not calm?" He asked jokingly.

"No, but it definitely sounds like something you would say."

He nodded in agreement and drank his coffee before turning to look at me. And there it was, that look. The one that he tried so hard to hide. The one that said he saw me and wanted more than just my body. The one that made my heart take flying leaps of faith and want to demand he love me, to never stop looking at me that way.

Then it was gone with a blink, but the smile remained.

"What are you going to do when you have kids and they're able to read these?" he asked after taking another drink.

He'd never even said the word *kids* around me. Maybe it was the high from that simple blip of a look, but my imagination shot off wondering how the conversation would go, and we'd talk about our possible kids and how amazing they'd be.

But I shut it down, and instead said, "Dunno. Tell them that I'm an adult and not to say those words."

He laughed. "Sounds like a solid plan."

"Well what would you do?" I asked, poking him in the chest.

"I don't know."

"See. You don't have a plan either."

"Nope." He stopped looking at me and stared at his coffee like he was hoping to find some tea leaves that would tell him his future. "Never figured I'd need one."

I hated that he looked away. My imagined conversation was vanishing quickly. "Why?"

"Never thought of having kids."

"Like at all?" I knew he was older and talked about how hard his job was, but it never crossed my mind that he just didn't *ever* want children. I figured he just hadn't found the right women, or the time to find that woman.

"Nope." His short answers should have been warning enough to not push it, but I just couldn't not know.

"What if you found a woman and married her and she wanted kids?" Insert me, our marriage, our kids.

"I'm not the marrying kind."

I had to laugh. I didn't know what he meant by that, but he looked pretty damn marry-able. "Why not?"

His chest heaved over a deep breath. "I'm thirty-eight, Juliana. Not exactly in my prime for marriage."

"You're not at death's door either."

I could hear my tone. I could hear his. This was no longer a hypothetical conversation. It was shifting, morphing. My morning coffee in bed with the man I fell in love with, was becoming an argument with a stiff stranger.

"I'm set in my ways and don't want to change. Don't want anything serious."

"Then what are *we* doing?"

There I said it. The gauntlet was down and watching his shoulders stiffen and his head slowly turn to me with confusion and irritation that he even had to explain, made me want to pick that gauntlet back up and swallow it whole.

"What do you mean what are we doing? We're fucking."

Those two words hit me like a one-two punch in the face and I jerked back at hearing them. How could he put it so simply? How could he pretend things hadn't changed from when we actually *were* just fucking? No. I wouldn't let him say that.

"We're more than just fucking and you know it."

"Juliana."

I ignored his warning, set my mug down and turned to face him again. Ready to make him admit it. Throwing it all out there, so he couldn't hide anymore.

"I see the way you look at me. I've felt the way you hold me. It's different than Jamaica or the first night I came to you. You know it is, so why can't you just admit it?"

He rubbed at his jaw line. "What do you want from me, Juliana?"

"I want to be with you. To keep doing what we're doing. Laughing, fucking, making love, sharing our lives. I want to go to Sunday brunch with you and sit next to you and hold your hand."

He gave me a warning look, like I should know better. It pissed me off. "Jack would kill-"

"Fuck my brother!" I shouted it, throwing my hands out to the side, moving to my knees so I could face him head-on. "You're thirty-eight, Shane. A man. One who doesn't apologize for anything. So, stop. Making. Excuses."

He moved to stand from the bed and reached down to grab his boxers. Once he had them in place, he began pacing and running his hand through his short hair. "You're right, Juliana. I'm a thirty-eight-year-old man who has a dangerous job and works a lot of hours. I don't want to bring anyone into that. There has been no one who was worth it."

I swallowed the pain of his words: *Not worth it.* It was another excuse. He knew it. I knew it. I scrambled through my thoughts to figure out why he was making so many damn excuses. And it hit me. I didn't know if it was true, but I'd find out when I let the words fly.

"You're scared." I said it softly, letting him know I didn't judge him. Leaving him an opening to confess to me and we could move forward.

Unfortunately, that was not the turn it took.

"I'm not fucking scared." He growled the words and stopped his pacing to point at me. Then he pulled his pants on and had his shirt in his hand. He was leaving and I wasn't ready yet. It sparked my anger that he'd try and walk out in the middle of this. It pissed me off seeing him put his shirt on, covering the chest I'd touched at my own leisure just last night. I hated that he would rather start a fight, deny, and make excuses than just simply admit what he felt

"You. Are. Scared." I didn't soften my words that time. His head popped out of his shirt and he opened his mouth to speak, but I wasn't done. "You have spent your whole life never feeling the way I make you feel. You never stayed in a home long enough to spark that kind of emotion. No woman has ever held on long enough. And you don't know what to do with it. You're scared of it."

His jaw clenched and his nostrils flared. If Shane had one thing in spades, it was pride, and his was coming out full force, not wanting to admit he'd never felt this before. Not wanting to even admit it existed within him. A part of me knew I'd pushed too far bringing up what he'd shared with me about his foster care, but I was tired of pretending.

When he smirked at me, I tried to prepare myself for the blow, but it was worse than I could have imagined.

"And you think you can? You think the little twenty-five-year-old girl who's in her first real job, still trying to be a big girl away from mommy and daddy, can change me?" He laughed with no humor. "I am who I am, *Mini MacCabe*, and you're just a child with hope in her eyes. Unwilling to see anything beyond what you want to happen. One breakdown away from running back home."

My anger burned the more his words sank into me, hitting every single weak spot he knew I had. Tears burned the backs of my eyes and it pissed me off even more. I'd trusted him. I'd *trusted* him, and he threw the weakest part of me back in my face. I could barely look at him.

"You're an asshole."

"I never said I wasn't."

Even with the tears building, I scoffed, letting my bitterness and pain slip into my words. Using condescending insults as my defense mechanism. "You want to tell me you're a *man* who is unchangeable, but all I can see is a fucking baby running scared."

"Real mature, Juliana. Way to use your big girl words."

I swallowed hard and had to look away as the first tears fell. "Get the fuck out."

I listened to every angry footstep as they got further and further away. I jerked, and let the first sob shake my chest when the door slammed.

Not a minute later, Jolene rushed into my room and threw her arms around me, soothing me, rubbing her hands up and down my shaking back.

"How? How did it spiral this far?" I kept sucking in short breaths, crying as I tried to understand how it fell apart so quickly. "I can't even remember how it started?"

"Shh. Shh. It's not your fault, Jules."

"Yes. It is. I pushed and I pushed and I . . ." My voice broke on another cry and I struggled to catch my breath. "I thought if I tried, he would just admit he cared. I hadn't expected a proclamation of love. I just wanted to know he cared. God, I was so mean. We were both so mean. And for what?"

"Stop, Jules. Just stop." She gripped my cheeks in her hands and made me look at her, making me hear her. "It's his loss if he can't see what an amazing woman you are. If he's too damn stubborn to try. You deserve more."

Did I? Right then, remembering how I brought up his upbringing and called him a baby, I sure as hell didn't feel like it.

Chapter Twenty

Praise Jesus I didn't have to go into the station on Monday. I couldn't have handled seeing him. I wasn't able to handle seeing anyone.

I'd laid around all day Saturday and avoided all the missed calls and messages on Sunday asking where I was when I hadn't shown for the Sunday brunch I'd promised I'd be at. I couldn't go.

I was too scared that Shane would be there. Fear that he wouldn't be there. My mind had already imagined showing up and him announcing his love for me for everyone to hear. But I shut it down faster than it formed. And I knew that no matter if he was there or not, I wouldn't have been able to hide my sadness.

God, I'd thought our relationship was going somewhere. Maybe I had been naive and the stupid little girl Shane had accused me of being. Either way, I hadn't been ready to face the masses.

However, Monday didn't care how I felt, I had a job to go to.

When I stepped off the elevator, I saw Dr. Voet unlocking his office. My shoes on the tile floor drew his attention and he looked back, smiling when he saw it was me.

"Hey, Juliana. How are you?"

"Morning, Dr. Voet. I'm okay. How are you?"

His blue eyes scanned my face and he smiled. "Better than you it seems." He held his door open for me. "Why don't you come in for a coffee? It's early still."

"Thank you, but I only drink iced coffee with an unhealthy amount of cream and sugar."

He laughed at my answer. "It's a good thing I have a fancy machine that makes iced coffee. And that I also have an unhealthy amount of cream and sugar. And chocolate."

"How can I turn that down?" I asked with a tired laugh.

I followed him into his secretary's office and then his own. I'd been in his office many times, but usually only for business meetings and such. This time felt a little different. More social.

He smiled more, kept looking back at me as the coffee brewed and he prepared the mugs. One said, *I use this mug periodically*, with a periodic table of elements. Then he handed me one that had a cartoon drawing of Neil DeGrasse Tyson that said, *Ya'll mothafuckas need science.*

I laughed and admitted to my own collection of mugs.

"Interesting for someone who doesn't drink hot coffee."

Immediately, my mind thought of Shane and how he'd said the same thing. Apparently, my face showed the pain that washed over me at the memory of us at Findlay's Market, because Dr. Voet stepped closer than normal and bent his knees to look into my downturned face.

"Hey, you okay?"

I had to swallow past the lump in my throat that his soft words caused. My heart was too sensitive, my emotions too close to the surface to handle such tenderness.

"Yeah." I somehow managed to choke the word out and tried to force a smile, only briefly letting my eyes connect with his before looking away.

I watched his hand lift toward my face as though in slow motion and my heart beat erratically in my chest. His fingers pushed my hair back, grazing my temple in the process and I couldn't help but stare at him with wide eyes. I knew it was inappropriate for work, for colleagues, for a boss and an employee, but not caring because I needed a tender touch just then.

"You sure?" he asked, moving his hand back from my face, the connection broken.

I tried to laugh, trying to lighten the tension that stretched taught between us. "Yeah. Just tired. I'm sure I look like hell for the amount of sleep I've gotten this weekend."

"Well, I think you always look beautiful."

I ducked, hiding the blush staining my cheeks. "Thank you."

I wanted his words to make me feel better. To know that a man still found me beautiful even if Shane didn't want me. But really, they just hurt. They hurt because they hadn't come from the man I wanted to hear them from.

That morning had ended up being the best part of the day since the rest declined rapidly when Dr. Stahl arrived in a mood that made his day-to-day rudeness seem pleasant. He blew past Jo and me sitting at our benches with a glare and no words. When the door slammed behind him to his office, both of us jumped at the loud bang that resonated around the room. I thought the glass beakers along the wall were going to come crashing to the ground.

Unfortunately, Jo left me alone soon after, giving me a sad smile. "I promise to be back soon. Hopefully, the Wicked Dick of the West stays in his office until his next class."

"Have fun teaching the kiddos in lab. Say a prayer and rush back to me soon."

She walked out the door with three fingers held high, a la *Hunger Games*.

I'd gotten through maybe half my procedure for the day when I heard the door to Dr. Stahl's office creak open.

"Juliana." His harsh voice cracked against my ears. "Go teach my class."

"But, I—"

"I didn't ask for your shit excuses. Just go do it."

My eyes wide behind my goggles, hand frozen on my pipette, I jumped when he slammed the door again. I didn't know how long I sat there trying to process the fact that my boss had just yelled at me. He was horrible, but not quite to the point of shouting and swearing at us.

Heat rushed from my neck and over my face. How dare he yell at me? I wanted to go in there and let him know he could shove his attitude up his ass, but when I glanced at the clock, I saw I only had five minutes before the lecture started. Taking a deep breath, I decided to be the bigger person and push it down.

I turned off all the machines and searched for the book for the semester, not even knowing what chapter they were working on. I'd have to check once I made it to the room and give the text a brief glance and hope for the best.

I'd stumbled through the lecture, knowing I sounded monotonous. Hell, half the class looked as if they were fighting sleep.

But whatever. Fuck it. I let them go early and prepared myself to get yelled at by Dr. Stahl when I showed up back to the lab thirty minutes early. But, when I walked in, his door was open and the room was empty. I breathed a sigh of relief for having dodged at least one bullet for the week.

Tuesday had me in the lab at the station. I'd remained glued to that room, not daring to walk out the door unless absolutely necessary. I packed my lunch and water bottle and pawned off running any errands to someone else. When I had a bathroom emergency, I mostly kept my head down and darted down the hall. Just as I was about to reach the restroom, I heard him and my eyes flicked up to see him talking to his partner. I panicked and walked into the first door on my left needing to get out of sight and found myself in a broom closet, where I proceeded to take deep breaths, and tried to control the tears burning the backs of my eyes. After probably too long, I snuck out and made a quick escape to the bathroom and then ran back to the lab.

Wednesday was a repeat of Monday with Dr. Voet. Instead of inviting me in his office for coffee, he'd stopped by Starbucks and brought me a hot chocolate, explaining that he wanted to cheer me up this week. When he'd complimented me again, it hurt less than Monday. Hopefully that meant Shane's hold on me was diminishing, but the words still didn't hit the spot.

Jolene walked around the corner just when his hand rested on my shoulder and slipped down my arm. She'd cocked an eyebrow in a *What the fuck is going on?* kind of way, and I shrugged. I honestly didn't know. It didn't stop her from giving me the third degree as soon as we walked into the lab.

"What the hell was that about?"

"I have no idea," I said, before taking a sip of my hot chocolate.

"Juliana."

"I swear. I honestly don't know what it's all about. He's just been . . .Really nice this week?" I finished the sentence on a question, unsure of how to explain it. "We ran into each other on Monday and he invited me into his office for coffee. I kind of assumed he wanted to talk about how the forensic stuff was going, but we just talked. Then he asked if I was okay. He also complimented me. And maybe he brushed my hair back." I shrugged.

"Maybe?" Jo asked incredulously.

"Maybe." I avoided her eyes and leaned over my bag to pull out my notebook.

"Well, he's hot as hell, so you can't be too sad about it."

"I'm not sad about it. Just confused. On top of everything else this week."

"Well, if you don't want him, you send him my way. He may be a professor, but I'll be sure to teach him a thing or two." She bobbed her eyebrows and made me laugh for the first time all week.

It was quickly squashed when Dr. Stahl came out of his office, slamming the door behind him. My eyes widened as he stomped closer to my bench. When he neared my workstation, he thrust a stack of papers toward me, shoving them into my line of sight.

"What the hell is this, Juliana?" His bushy eyebrows lowered over his dark eyes. His nose flared over a pinched frown.

"Uhh." I stuttered over my answer, trying to regroup before eventually looking at the form. "It looks like the shipping form for this week's deliveries."

"And whose signature is that?" His finger stabbed at the bottom of the paper.

"Mine. I was the only one in the lab when the products were delivered on Monday."

"And what is this?" He flipped a new page to the front.

I looked it over, getting frustrated with the twenty questions. "The sign-in sheet for the storage room."

"The sheet we're supposed to fill out when we take the deliveries to the storage room, so we know who is accountable for what."

"Yeah," I answered confused. I didn't know why he was recapping such basic instructions.

"Then where the hell is your signature? And why are there a slew of chemicals missing from the storage area that were delivered on Monday? Where is the disconnect here?"

"What?" My heart pounded in my chest as he threw questions at me. It felt like an accusation, but my mind was stumbling to keep up with what he was saying. "But I signed everything in."

"Did you? I had to suffer the embarrassment of a *lab manager* coming to me and reprimanding *me* about procedures of signing materials in and out." He dragged out *lab manager*, like the words were disgusting on his tongue. "Do you know how embarrassing that was? Especially with the dean of the department standing right there to witness it all."

"I . . . I—"

Those are expensive chemicals, Ms. MacCabe. What were you doing with them?"

My cheeks burned with panic. Was he accusing me of stealing? Why would I do that? What the hell was happening? He needed to believe me. "I signed them in." I tried to make my voice stronger, but it came out high and reedy.

"Come with me, Ms. MacCabe. We will go to the dean with this issue of theft."

He stormed out, his white lab coat fanning behind him. I looked to Jo and her eyes were just as wide with confusion as mine.

"Jo, I didn't . . ." I swallowed past the lump in my throat trying to push back the burn in my eyes. I needed to walk into that office calmly and not be all emotional.

"I know. Just go talk to Dr. Voet, and it will get sorted out."

I fumbled out of my chair and rushed down the hall to Dr. Voet.

"Dr. Stahl, obviously there was a mistake and as I said before, we will look into the situation." Dr. Voet's calm voice reached outside the office and when I walked through the door, it was to Dr. Stahl looming over the dean's desk and Dr. Voet leaning back in his chair, relaxed and unconcerned.

"What do you mean *look into it*?" He shook the papers between them. "The proof is right here. What more do you need?"

"We need to consider everything. More than just one missing signature."

"Let me look into it. It's my lab and my incompetent research associate. I'll deal with her."

"The department can deal with the issue. But thank you for offering."

Dr. Voet met my eyes when I walked in and gave me a small, almost undetectable nod. It eased only the slightest pinch in my chest, but the vice was still there squeezing the breath from my lungs. Dr. Stahl turned to see me walk in and scowled. As I got closer, I could see sweat beading at his temples he was so worked up.

"It's because she's a woman, isn't it? Women shouldn't be in the science lab. Men are too soft on them."

"Enough, Professor." Dr. Voet's voice rang with authority.

Dr. Stahl's jaw clenched and he turned, scowling at me as he walked past, muttering "Women shouldn't be in the science lab. Men are too soft on them."

Once he cleared the door, Dr. Voet seemed to let out a breath he'd been holding and ran a hand over his hair, pulling his thick-rimmed glasses off.

"I'm sorry about this, Juliana."

"I don't know what happened. I signed for the delivery into the lab and took them straight to storage where I signed them in. I don't—"

He was shaking his head before I even finished. "Don't worry. We'll figure it out."

I took a deep, shaky breath and nodded my head.

"You can head home for the rest of the day. Not as a punishment," he rushed to finish when he saw my eyes widen in fear of being reprimanded and banished from the lab.

"I, um . . .I have a procedure I'm in the middle of. I can't leave it."

"Sure, sure. I just didn't want you to feel uncomfortable with Dr. Stahl today."

I chuckled softly. "When are we not uncomfortable around him?"

"True." He laughed at my joke and before we said goodbye, he told me to come to him with any issues and promised to keep me informed on whatever they found.

It didn't really settle anything and the stress of the day caused me to mess up my procedure twice. Rather than waste anymore materials, I caved and left the lab an hour early. Jo gave me a sad smile and told me we'd order pizza when she got home.

Thursday was another day to add to the shit-show I called my life. I'd woken up late and had to rush to the station, forgetting my lunch. I tried to hold strong and just go without lunch, but my stomach grumbled on repeat for a solid hour and the technicians were looking at me like an alien was about to pop out of my stomach. Then my hands got too shaky to pipette and that was the final straw. I needed to at least grab a bag of chips. It was late anyway.

No one is going to be there. He won't be there. It will be fine.

I said it on repeat when I walked the halls, looking left and right like I was escaping prison.

I arrived to a cafeteria that was much busier than I expected, but hoped the crowd would hide me. I was standing in line, two away from ordering my sandwich at the little kiosk, when I saw him. He stood by the door talking to his partner, his profile so beautiful and hitting me right in the chest. As though he could feel my stare, his head turned and his eyes met mine. He was too far away for me to read his expression, but his eyes lingered on me longer than a glimpse.

My heart kicked up in my chest and the world got quiet, my blood pumping in my ears the only sound around me.

Did he miss me?

Did he want to run across the room and pull me into a kiss?

Did he want to proclaim his love right then and there?

Then his partner slapped him on his shoulder and drew his attention away, the moment broken. All my foolish imaginations crumbled and I resigned myself to the fact he was probably staring at my boobs the whole time. My heart fell to my feet and being a glutton for punishment, I stared a little longer.

I missed him.

And it hurt.

"Hell of a man, amiright?" My attention jerked to the petite blonde standing next to me, also staring at Shane with a small smile that said she would strip for him if he'd asked. She leaned in closer to me. "Between us women, he fucks like a freight train, too."

She nudged me with her elbow and smiled before stepping up to the counter to order. Frozen, I stood there watching this woman order her sandwich. Wondering what she shared with Shane. Wondering how many others there were. Wondering why I thought I was different.

I was no longer hungry. My stomach pitched, and I swallowed hard, looking over to where Shane was, the spot now empty. I stumbled out of the cafeteria, back to the lab on auto pilot, barely functioning through the motions, screwing up more procedures again.

God, I was such a mess.

Deciding not to waste the department's materials, I filled out paperwork and oversaw other's work until it was time to go.

My body felt both hollow and heavy. I wanted to cry and do nothing. All of it tugging at my insides.

I felt some relief at making it through the day, at least until I drove home and Betsy broke down half-way there. I managed to get her off to the side of the road where I screamed and sobbed and beat my steering wheel. So mad at my damn car for betraying me too this week. I let it all out, steaming up the windows with the amount of heat my anger produced.

Once I'd finished, I dug my phone out of my purse and called the insurance company, knowing what to do after Shane had helped me last time. The driver came and towed my car to a shop. He was even nice to offer me a ride home and didn't ask any questions about why my eyes were so red.

He let me stare out the window and only gave me a nod when I muttered my thanks. Probably realizing what a lost cause I was.

Friday, I used a sick day to wallow on the couch, eat ice cream and take-out, and feel sorry for myself. I didn't shower. I didn't brush my teeth. And I ignored all messages on my phone.

Saturday, I repeated it all over again.

Chapter Twenty-One

Sunday, I finally decided to get up and out of my wallowing.

And by decided, I meant that Jo came into my room with a mug of iced coffee that read, *I ain't no baby bitch.* She plopped down heavily on my bed, making me bounce, and let me know I was starting to stink.

I gave her a strong side-eye, letting her know I didn't appreciate her honesty and reached for the mug. I turned on the television in my room and we watched a morning game show as we finished our drinks without talking.

"You smell like a stinky hobo," she said once the show had ended.

"You're too sweet, Jo."

"Just keeping it real." She turned to look at me with sad, but hard eyes. "You know we don't need to talk about it. I know enough to hurt with you. But no matter the hurt, you need to get up and bathe yourself. Otherwise, I will be forced to either dump a bucket of water on you, or kick you out. I can't be having that kind of stank lingering when I bring my future husband over."

"Wouldn't want to ruin your prospects. That's the only reason I'll shower. Because you need to find a husband before your family kidnaps you and marries you off to their idea of a 'good man'."

"Anything but that." She shifted to face me, her eyes pleading. "Please bathe so I can choose my own husband."

"Okay, but just for you."

She fell back on the bed dramatically, arms thrown up in victory. My eyes burned then because it hit me how lucky I was to have her. She didn't need to have a conversation about what was wrong with me. She let me be a stinky hobo until it was enough, and then called me out in a roundabout way that made me laugh for the first time in a few days.

I patted her hand and then rolled out of bed, grabbing my clothes and heading to the shower. When I was clean again, I walked into the living area, and she didn't even look up from the magazine she was flipping through when she announced, "We're going to Sunday brunch."

"No."

Page flip. "Yes."

"Jo."

Page flip. "Yes."

"I don't wa-"

Her head finally lifted and she stared me down, interrupting me firmly. "Yes!"

Narrowing my eyes, I tried to hold strong. She gave me a bored stare, unamused with my weak glare. Finally, I caved and rolled my eyes. "Fine."

Her lips curled and she wore a victorious smile before returning to her magazine. "It will be good for you. And I'm in the mood for some delicious free food."

While we waited until it was time to leave, we watched another game show, because we were super productive like that, and she caught me up on Dr. Stahl during the commercials. Apparently, he'd been on a ragey bender and even yelled at a couple of students in the lab for the mistakes they were making. Not even an advanced lab, but the lab for non-chemistry majors. He'd made a big hoopla about having been assigned to teach the class, saying it was beneath him, although every teacher did their rounds teaching it.

Listening to her tell me how one girl left crying and headed to the dean's office, made me feel a little bit better about skipping Friday. Although I felt bad for leaving Jo to deal with it all.

I headed to my room to finish getting dressed when my phone rang. My heart jumped into my throat, and I hated myself for scrambling to get it, hoping it would be Shane. I was an idiot and a glutton for punishment.

It was my mom. Just seeing her name made me eager to talk to her after such a shit week.

"Hey, Mama."

"Hey baby. You sound sad," she said in her soft Southern accent.

Mama knew me better than anyone, which is why it was so easy for her to read me in only two words. I wished she could coddle me like she did when I was younger. I swallowed the lump trying to make its way up my throat and worked to get a half-lie out.

"I'm just tired. It's been stressful at work and my boss is kind of being a dick, which makes it worse."

"Well, no one is a dick to my baby girl."

I snorted at hearing my mom say *dick*. A Southern belle never said such vulgar words. "Thanks, Mama."

She laughed with me before getting serious. "Enough with the giggles. What's going on?"

I wanted to admit everything to her. Fall at her feet and beg her to hold me. But I left claiming how strong and independent I was, and falling apart now would let her know I was failing. And while my mom was the most supportive of my family, she'd latch on to it and use it as reasons to get me back home. So, I settled on a vague truth.

"Just . . .Just some boy troubles."

"Oh, baby. What happened?

"Nothing." I didn't want to have to explain everything, it would only make it worse. I just wanted the comfort from her.

"You want me to tell your father?" she joked. "You just give me that boy's name."

Her joke worked, because I imagined my mom marching up to my father and demanding he do something about a boy who made her little girl sad. "No, don't tell Daddy. He'd tell me if I was in Texas, I wouldn't have to worry. That no Southern gentleman would break my heart, and then he'll push for me to come home."

Her deep breath reached me over the line. "He just wants what's best for you."

"And you? Do you think Texas is best for me? Do you think giving up what I love to stand at a man's side and run charities is best for me?"

I knew she thought being close to her in Texas was best, but hoped she'd maybe softened her stance on it. She had been more understanding than Daddy had been, but still rooted in tradition.

"I knew you needed space, Juliana. You always were so stubborn, demanding to do everything yourself. But you can't blame me for wanting to keep my baby close. We just want our little girl to be taken care of. Especially if something should ever happen to us."

It was an argument I'd heard before. My parents were older. They'd had Jack when they were in their late thirties and then I came as a surprise. They'd done all the treatments to get pregnant with Jack and got lucky early on. After him, it took a lot longer for her to get pregnant again. When they'd finally given up, I came along.

I was the little girl they never thought they'd get. I tried to understand, but when I was suffocating under the pressure, it was hard to see it from their perspective.

"I know, Mama," I said, even if I didn't.

"I hate that you're hurting alone."

Her soft words caused a burn behind my eyelids. I hadn't had many heartbreaks when I first started dating. Then early on, I'd gone steady with Hudson, but when I had the occasional upset, she'd always been there. I missed her now.

"I'm not alone." I tried to reassure her and myself. "I have Jolene."

"Have you told Jack?"

"God no. He's almost worse than dad when it comes to me dating."

She laughed remembering all the times Jack would come back from the Army to warn off the guys at school with his presence alone.

"I'm going to brunch in a bit, so I won't be alone. You don't need to worry."

Before we ended the call, she brought up one last thing that made me cringe. "You know, Hudson's been asking about you more."

Hudson had been messaging me on and off. A mix between doubtful messages, checking in, and sweet words, talking about memories of good times and how it could be that good again. But I'd been so busy that I hadn't taken him too seriously or really paid him any attention.

For a moment, at the mention of his name, I missed him. I missed being wanted by someone as much as Hudson seemed to want me.

"Hudson should know better," I said, trying to deter my mom from hoping for anything between us. I missed him, but it was more of a moment of sadness rather than actually wanting him.

"That boy is just as stubborn as you are."

"We did butt heads more often than not," I said, laughing at the memories of us as kids. "But, Mama, Hudson's not what I want anymore, and no amount of stubbornness will change that."

"I know, baby." She sounded resigned, but still my sympathetic mom.

"I'm sorry I'm not coming home. I'm sorry I can't be the woman you raised me to be."

"Juliana," she reprimanded. "You know we always love you. You get your stubbornness from your father. And sooner or later he will come around and express how proud he is of you. He's a sore loser and you're his baby. He wanted to do everything he could to keep you close."

"Including doubting me? Pushing his expectations on me?" My bitterness at his lack of support slipped through my words.

"We both love you. And your father never doubted you. I think that's what scared him the most, why he fought so hard to make you stay. Because he knew once you left, that you would figure out how successful you could be on your own two feet."

I didn't know what to say to that. Maybe I'd struggled to see past my determination to prove him wrong. Maybe I'd let my bitterness over how he'd shunned my need to be my own person, that I didn't remember the supportive man who raised me my whole life. My mother was right. I did get my stubbornness from him.

"I love you, Mama."

"We love you too."

Swallowing past the lump in my throat, I looked up at a Jolene grabbing her things and getting ready to go.

"Hey, Mama. I have to get going. I'll tell Jack you said hi."

"Okay, baby. Call me if you need me. Give Lu a kiss for me."

"I will. Bye."

I hung up and stared at the phone, feeling better for having talked to my mom and worse because she always reminded me how much they wanted me home.

And there were times this week when heading home hadn't sounded so horrible.

On a whim of homesickness, I pulled up Hudson's name and quickly sent a message before we left. I didn't think about the implications. I just thought of the best memory I wanted to remember at that moment. One that reminded me of how it felt to not feel so hollow.

Me: Remember that night we took a joy ride around the golf course in the cart, and we stopped to watch the stars just to get caught by the sprinklers? I laughed so hard that night.

Me: Just reminiscing. I miss talking and laughing with my friend.

⸙

Brunch was a struggle. It hurt to laugh and I had to force every smile.

"What's wrong with you," Jack asked. Apparently I hadn't been hiding my pain well enough.

"I'm just tired."

"Well, that sucks Jules. Try getting more sleep." Unlike my mom, Jack believed my lie. Although, I had to fight to keep from rolling my eyes at his lame suggestion.

"Thanks for that sage advice. I never thought of getting more sleep," I deadpanned. "On top of it all, work is a fucking mess."

"A mess is an understatement," Jolene muttered.

"What's going on," Luella asked.

I broke down what had happened at the lab and everything with Dr. Stahl.

"What a dick," Evie said, mirroring my mom's words.

"I can't believe he'd try and pin something like that on you." Luella said around a clenched jaw. "I'm sure they'll get to the bottom of it, Jules."

"Thanks guys."

"Maybe I can have Shane look into it." Jack said

I cringed just hearing his name.

"I mean, obviously there's some criminal activity. I'm sure he knows someone."

"Yeah." I choked the word out. Jack didn't seem to notice or care, but when I looked up, I met Evie's shrewd gaze. Swallowing hard, I looked away. I didn't need anyone digging deeper than what I'd told them.

I sat through the rest of lunch waiting for someone to say his name again. Thankfully, I didn't have to hear it again and hide my reaction, but Evie's gaze never wavered from scrutinizing me. After I helped clean up and grabbed my purse, I waited for her to approach me and ask what was going on, but it never came.

When I fell in to my seat in Jo's car, she looked at me and said my two favorite words. "Alcohol store."

Which brought us to strolling through the aisles, trying to decide between a pinot grigio or a chardonnay, or to just say fuck it and throw back vodka-cranberries until our heads pounded from the alcohol and sugar rush. Each option had its own merits.

We were discussing whether Chinese or Mexican went best with wine and vodka when our cart bumped into another, the bottles clanking against the metal like a car accident. Jo looked like she was about to rip into the person when suddenly, her eyes widened and she smiled.

"Oh, hey, Dr. Voet."

I jerked my head from Jo to Dr. Voet, who stood tall, holding only one bottle of wine as opposed to our seven in the cart. Obviously, some of us were thirstier than others.

"Hey, Dr. Voet."

"Hello, ladies. And please, call me Calvin," he said as he looked over the contents we were pushing around. "You having a party?"

"Nope. Just your typical weekly shopping trip," Jo joked. Thankfully he laughed and didn't assume we were a pair of raging alcoholics. "We're just having a girls' night, soothing our woes of Dr. Stahl."

"Jo." I tried to reprimand her under my breath and remind her this was the head of our department.

However, Dr. Voet—I mean Calvin—laughed and gave a knowing shrug, before turning to me and looking me over.

"I hope you're feeling better, Juliana."

"Yes, thank you."

Jo, the traitorous friend she was, abandoned ship. "Hey, I'm just going to go check out that other wine that we were talking about. The one with the alcohol."

I watched her walk away, holding off finally meeting the dean's eyes. When I caved and peeked up at him beneath my lashes, he had a soft, knowing smile.

"She's not very subtle."

I laughed. "That she is not."

"I can't blame her, I'm not very subtle when I want something either." His eyes looked over my face, as though caressing my skin. "You look much more rested. Still just as beautiful."

I swallowed hard and ducked my head to hide the blush staining my cheeks. "Thank you."

Licking my lips nervously, I searched for something else to say, but the only thing I could focus on was the way my heart seemed to be trying to pound out of my chest. I struggled to decipher the emotions coursing through me. Was I excited? Was I nervous? I think I was mostly scared because it was a final step toward letting Shane go.

"I know we work together, Juliana, but I'm not directly your boss, and there's no rules against dating. We're both adults, and I was wondering if I could take you on a date next weekend."

"Ummm . . ." I think I knew the question was coming, but I still stuttered over a response, unprepared. I opened my mouth, hoping the right answer would tumble out, when he stopped me.

"Just think about it. Let me know tomorrow."

He squeezed my shoulder and let his hand slide down my arm. I nodded like a bobble head and watched him walk to the check out.

As though she was watching the whole thing around the corner, Jo popped out and hopped from one foot to the other.

"What the hell happened? Tell me everything."

I laughed at her excitement. "He asked me on a date."

"He what?" She whisper-screamed and I had to shush her, looking over my shoulder to see who had heard.

"I can't, Jo. I'm not really ready and we work together. And what if it didn't work? Then it would be awkward."

Her eyebrow raised a little higher with each excuse that tumbled from my lips. "Jules. You better accept that damn date. He is hot, and I expect you to do it for me. I need to live vicariously through you, because that man is delicious."

"Ugh."

"Don't you roll your eyes at me." She pointed her finger at me. "You will. You at least have to try."

"Jo."

"Do. It. Dooo it," she said.

"Fine. Damn. I'll let him know tomorrow."

"Hell, no. He's just now checking out. Go. Tell him now."

"Jol-"

"Now!" She turned my shoulders and shoved me away.

I hurried my steps as I saw him grab his bag and head toward the door.

"Dr. Voet," I called out.

He turned and smiled at my approach. "Calvin, please."

"Calvin." I had to admit I liked the way his name sounded on my lips. "I actually don't need until tomorrow. I'd love to go on a date with you."

His smile lit up his face, and I had to admit it was nice to see someone so excited to sit across a table and just talk to me. Get to know me, and want me for more than just sex.

"Fantastic. Next Friday. I'll make a reservation and pick you up at six."

"Six." Walking backwards, I nodded and smiled a genuine smile. Nerves ran a riot through my body. Maybe I was making a mistake accepting a date so soon. But I also felt a little lighter trying to take a step in a better direction toward getting over Shane.

Chapter Twenty-Two

"You can drop me off right here." I pointed to the front of my building.

He pulled up to the curb and parked. "Let me grab your door."

Watching Calvin walk around the car he was tall, broad, sexy, and smart. What more could a girl want? Dinner had been great. Filled with conversation and laughter. We'd talked about research, compared undergrad stories and how we got to where we were. He told me about the time in his graduate program where him and his buddies caught a whole lab bench on fire. I told him how I'd created a minor explosion in the chemical hood.

It had been nice to share that kind of connection with someone. Someone who respected my brain and didn't look at me as a cute little girl, playing at being an adult. Someone who didn't look at me like they were trying to appease my desire to be a scientist. He'd smiled when I'd told him my accomplishments, touched my hand through dinner. I'd watched his long tan fingers stroke from my wrist to my fingers where he slid his hand under mine to hold it.

I waited for the excited sparks to race up and jolt my heart into an excited thump. But they never came. How could I sit there with someone who respected me so much and look at me with such warmth, and yet still feel this empty, pinching pain for someone who didn't want me?

Calvin opened my door and held out his hand. I grabbed it and stood then pulled away, holding both my hands around my clutch in front of me.

"I had a great time tonight, Juliana."

"Me too. I needed all that laughter."

"Any time you need me to tell you about my crazy mistakes, just let me know. I'm happy to regale you with many more from my past."

I laughed and looked up into his dark blue eyes. My smile dropped as I watched his hand lift toward my face and brush a loose strand back behind my ear. He stepped closer and I quickly ran through my options. I imagined him leaning down to press his lips to mine, igniting the fire I'd been waiting for. I'd drop my clutch and wrap my arms around him. He'd lift me up and we'd go inside where he would ravish me all night, and I would feel whole again. I would feel happy.

Instead he leaned in and kissed my cheek, and I only felt his lips on my skin. No heat spread through me. No imagination came to life.

He pulled back and I smiled, but I think he saw that lack of feeling. He smiled back, but his eyes looked resigned, like he knew it would be our last date.

"Goodnight, Juliana."

"Goodnight, Calvin."

He got into his car and I walked toward my door, waving at him as he drove away. Just as I turned to mount the steps a shadowy figure stepped into the light.

"Cute date."

I screamed before I could control myself and pressed my hand to my chest, trying to coax it back to safe levels.

"What the *hell*, Shane? You almost gave me a fucking heart attack."

"Sorry, I didn't want to interrupt your farewells, so I waited my turn."

I looked at him, leaning against the lamp post. One ankle crossed over the other, jeans and a long sleeve shirt encasing his large body. His icy eyes seemed to glow under the light.

The fire I'd waited to feel with Calvin came flooding over my body at just Shane's presence and it pissed me off. I marched over to him and jabbed my finger into his chest.

"What the hell do you think you're doing here? I thought you didn't waste time with little girls," I said, throwing his cruel words back in his face.

He didn't respond like I wanted him to. He stood there and let his eyes scan me from my high heels to my skater skirt and blouse, until he lingered a long while at my lips. Everywhere his eyes touched, I burned, hotter than I'd been since that final night in his arms.

"I was sitting at a stop light, minding my own business, and there you are at a table in a restaurant, laughing with another man who was stroking your hand." Shane stood to his full height and took a step into me, so close there was only a small breath of space between us. "Did he kiss you? Does he know that wine tastes so much richer from your tongue?"

"You don't get to be jealous."

"I know I don't. And yet, here I am." He lifted his arms wide like he was just as baffled as I was that he stood before me, unsure of his real reason to be there.

"Why?" I asked again, trying to understand.

"I can't stop thinking about your kiss, your taste, and it kills me at the thought of him—or anyone that's not me—having it."

It was all about my body. He didn't miss me as a woman, the one he held at night, the one he laughed with. He missed my body. His pride the only driving force for him to be there. It sparked my anger, the heat rising in my cheeks, my blood boiling, looking for an outlet.

"I offered it to you." I was close to shouting, the emotions flooding me becoming too much. "I wanted to give it all to you and you turned me away."

"Juliana . . ." His shoulders dropped on a heavy sigh, almost like he was bored with my need for more. I wanted to scream at him. Hate him for standing there, and even as he rejected me, he turned me on more than my amazing date tonight.

I stepped forward and jabbed him in the chest. "Well, you can just go fuck your-"

His mouth crashed down on mine, stealing the words from my tongue with his own. I wanted to shove him away, finish telling him to go fuck himself.

Instead, I pressed my body to his. Moaned when his arms wrapped around my waist, grinding his cock against me. Wound my arms around his neck and dug my fingers into his short hair.

I tangled my tongue with his and nipped at his lips, wanting him to hurt a little, even if I also wanted to make him feel good. He grunted and began walking me backward. I didn't know where, but at that moment I would have followed him to the depths of hell if I could still feel his body pressed to mine.

The light from the street lamp disappeared as we worked our way into the darkness, until the rough brick of my building pressed into my back. His hands slid down over my hips, gripping my ass, lifting me onto my toes so he could grind his dick against my core.

His lips slid down my neck, biting, sucking, desperate for more. The sound of my moans were swallowed up by the night, and as his mouth worked its way between my breasts, I knew the moment to stop this was now or never. We were hidden in the dark alleyway of my building and the next. I needed to stop this. I even opened my mouth to say something. Stop, maybe?

All that escaped was a gasp when he nipped at my nipple over my shirt.

Instead, I dropped my hand to grip the hard length pressing against his jeans, loving the moan he let out against my skin. Loving the way he filled my hand, wanting him to fill my pussy.

I worked the button and zipper down and shoved my hand into his pants as his worked their way under my skirt, under my panties. His large fingers slid between the lips of my cunt.

"So wet. All for me." His words were deep and soft against my neck.

When his fingers glided over my clit, I squeezed his cock and he groaned. He removed my hand from his pants and I wanted to whimper at the loss of soft skin, but he turned me toward the wall, pressed my hands flat to the brick, and flipped my skirt over my ass.

I closed my eyes, rubbing myself against the roughness of his denim. I focused on the way the cool breeze of the night rushed past my heated skin. I heard the crinkle of a condom wrapper and his moan as he slipped it on.

Fingers worked at my panties, shoving them to the side, before he pressed the tip of his cock to my opening and began pushing in. A week I'd been empty without him, but it might as well have been years for as desperate as I felt to have him inside me again. I shoved back and we both let out guttural groans that we tried to stifle. It wasn't very late, and if someone heard us, they would look into the dark and see two lovers pressed together, frantic to be closer.

Shane wrapped his body around mine, one hand palming my breast, rubbing his thumb over my nipple and the other between my legs, touching my clit, feeling the way he slid in and out of me. His thrusts were frenzied and hard, each one causing a whimper to escape. I had to bite my lip to hold back the groan when his fingers moved in circles around my bundle of nerves, pushing me closer and closer to the edge.

"I missed your moans when I'm inside you. Nothing like it." His words were spoken into the back of my neck. The breath of them chilling against the sweat building there. "Missed the soft skin beneath my hands. Missed your taste, your lips."

Tears burned the backs of my eyes. It was all too much. The feel of him around me, inside me. His words telling me how much he missed my body. The pain that not one miss had been for me as a woman. My heart expanded and shrank in on itself all at once, trying to decide whether to burst with hope or hide in fear of getting hurt.

"Juliana. Juliana." He chanted my name.

"I miss you." I breathed the words to the ground, unsure if he even heard them.

But I did. I missed him so much. The tears coated my eyes and spilled down my cheeks, falling onto the ground at my feet.

"Come for me, baby. Let me feel your cunt squeezing me. Let me come in you."

His fingers pinched my nipple and worked my clit harder and faster, his thrusts changing their angle to hit me deeper and I had to use one hand to cover my mouth to soften the whimpering moans I couldn't control. He pushed in harder, further than before and bit into my shoulder to hide his own groans. But I felt them in my soul and they pulled more spasms from my core. I wanted it to last, scared of what the end of the moment meant.

He stayed inside me even after we were both done. I moved my hand back to the wall, needing to hold myself up. My legs were like Jell-O and my body weighed heavy with the fear of what was about to come. I tried to conjure the perfect picture in my imagination. The one where he would come upstairs with me and make love to me all night long. The one where he would go to Sunday brunch with my hand in his. The one where we're together.

But I knew—I just knew—that it wasn't going to happen and more tears slipped out. The hopeful little girl he accused me of being couldn't give up without using every last bit of fight in my arsenal. So, I said the words. I gave him everything and prayed he'd take it. Even if he didn't, at least I'd said my peace.

"I love you."

His whole body froze around me, still inside me. A minute on a precipice wondering which way I'd fall. It lasted forever. His arms tightened around me, his cock pushing in a little further even while softening, and the breath he'd been holding gusted out against my skin.

And then he released me, pulling out. "I have to go."

I swallowed back the lump in my throat, keeping my position against the wall. Letting my fingers dig into the brick, trying to gain my composure before I turned to face him. Trying to fight off the hurt and anger filling me up. I didn't even know which one filled me more. Hurt? Anger? Fight to win? Sulking away in loss? I wanted to slam my fist against the wall to release some of them.

Instead, I stood up and my skirt fell over my bottom again, my core clenching in emptiness, and I turned to face him where he was avoiding my eyes and fastening his pants.

While he looked away, I wiped my cheeks discreetly and struggled to find the words, but I didn't know what to say. I didn't know anything and I hated it.

"Why?" I didn't even know what why I was asking about. Why he came? Why he fucked me? Why he wouldn't be with me? All of them?

He looked up and his eyes looked tired. Dark circles made the light blue stand out even more. But even the color looked dull. "I'm sorry."

His words hit me in the chest and the burning behind my eyes came on full force again. My breaths seemed to be trying to keep up with my pounding heart and the need to fight to win won out. At least for now. "Tell me you don't care about me," I pleaded.

He stared, seeming to weigh his words. "Of course, I care about you. You're Jack's little sister. He's my brother and I'd always protect you for him."

My heart rose and then plummeted to my feet, like a sick roller coaster ride.

"I am *not* some little girl you need to protect." I growled at him, angry that it was back to this bullshit excuse again. My shoulders heaved up and down with my angry breaths, fists clenching at my sides. "I am a woman you have made love to. I'm your equal."

"Juliana, don't be naive and make this into something it's not." He couldn't even meet my eyes when he said it. I watched his jaw clench and his throat bob over every swallow, like he was holding back words.

Why? Why wouldn't he just give in?

Irritated, I let out a low growl, barely holding back the need to be the petulant child he accused me of being and stomping my foot. "I am an adult, Shane." I was tired of explaining it, of defending my maturity. "One who can face the things in front of me. And I'm not the one who's afraid of admitting how much I love you."

I said it again, apparently a glutton for punishment. Watching him stiffen every time I said it.

He dropped his gaze, looking at the ground and shaking his head. The yoyo of emotions exhausted me and the tears were winning. They choked me and cracked my voice when all I wanted was to sound firm. "Don't shake your head at me." A tear leaked free and I sniffed again. "Shane." His name the final plea on my lips.

He lifted his head and met my wet eyes. For a moment, I was able to see him. He looked just as miserable as me, and I thought he was going to finally give in. He looked me over with his eyebrows scrunched together. He looked just as hollow as I felt.

Then he looked away, paced two steps away and then back, rubbed his hand over his neck, his head, his mouth. When his eyes looked back to meet mine, the hollowness was gone. And all that greeted me was a blank wall.

His voice was just as empty as his eyes, void of all emotions. "I know you think Jack has nothing to do with this, but he is my brother. He has become my family, and I am *not* willing to risk that on something as flimsy as a love proclamation. It's not worth it."

Not worth it.

Not worth it.

I'm not worth it.

My love wasn't worth it.

Holding back the tears was useless. I dropped my head and did the best I could to wipe them away, but sobs shook my body the more I tried to hold them in. His feet shuffled against the pavement as he stepped closer to me. Out of the corner of my eyes I saw his hand lift toward me.

Jerking my head up, I slapped his hand away. "Don't *touch* me." My voice cracked and I worked to harden it, to let my anger fill it. "Don't *ever* touch me. I don't need your comfort. I don't *need* you." He flinched at my words and the hard wall slipped a little, reveling how my words hit him. "I don't need someone who shows up to make me feel like a piece of meat."

He stepped forward again. "Juliana, I-"

I stepped back. "Don't."

Regret shined in his eyes, but I didn't care. It may not have been his intention to make me feel so cheap, but he had, and I felt no sympathy for him hurting from his actions.

"Go Shane. And don't ever come back here."

Chapter Twenty-Three

I turned my back on Shane and held my head high all the way to the entryway of my building. I'd even managed to seem more pissed than upset until the elevator doors closed. Just in case he'd watched me through the glass front of my building.

But as soon as those doors closed, I caved in on myself. My hands came up to cradle my face as my shoulders and head dropped down and loud sobs filled the small space. If anyone got on this elevator with me, I was fucked.

Praise Jesus, the elevator dinged on my floor and slid open to an empty hallway. I rushed to my apartment, fumbled with the key and fell against the door as soon as it was closed behind me, sliding down to my bottom.

I fully expected Jo to come storming out of her room demanding what the hell happened, but the place was dark and no one came for me. I sat, alone, on my apartment floor crying like a weak child. Maybe moving to Cincinnati was a mistake. It all felt like a giant joke right then.

My life in Texas had been good. Much better than the mess it felt like now. The guy I'd fallen in love with let me know I wasn't worth it. Betsy was a traitorous hunk of metal. And I was currently being accused of stealing materials from my lab.

All of it weighed on me, and it was so easy to allow the sadness to swallow me whole. But it was just a moment in my life. Just one week. I tried to be rational, knowing that it hadn't always been like that. I tried to remember all the reasons I loved it here.

But the hurt whispered to me. *What if it isn't just a moment? What if I just keep fucking up? Maybe I should just go home. My parents were right. Hudson was right.*

I wouldn't have to worry about being looked down upon in my job. I wouldn't have to worry about my car breaking down. I wouldn't have to worry about a broken heart. In our circle of friends in Texas, the men were gentlemen, and Daddy was not a man you crossed by hurting his baby girl. The men didn't take a woman they cared about to an alley to fuck her and leave her aching between your legs.

My legs clenched around the ache now and it sent a shock of pain and pleasure through me.

Picking myself off the floor, I made my way to the bathroom where I splashed cold water on my face. I stared at my reflection in the mirror, looking for answers that seemed so far out of reach. I was patting away the smudged make-up when I heard a knock at the door.

My skin prickled and my heart hammered against my chest.

Maybe it was Shane coming back to say what a huge mistake he'd made and that I was worth it, that he wanted the same things I did. I'd open the door and he'd pull me into his arms, whispering into my ear how much he loved me and tell me he wouldn't leave me. My eyes sparked with a hope I hated myself for having. I breathed in as deeply as my chest would allow and tried to be rational.

The knock came again and I rushed out of the bathroom to answer the door. My fingers fumbled with the locks as I bit my lips nervously. Flinging the door open, my heart dropped and my body tried to make sense of what was in front of me.

"Hudson." I breathed out his name in shock.

Disappointment settled around me as I took in the sweater over his polo, his dark hair perfectly parted and slicked back, his blue eyes, ten shades too dark. None of it was what I had wanted to greet me on the other side of my door.

"Hey, Jules." His easy smile slid from his face when he took in my puffy, red-rimmed eyes. His hands slipped from his pockets and he stepped into my space, pulling me to his chest. "Hey, hey. What happened? Why have you been crying?"

Because it was Hudson, the boy I'd grown up with, who knew so much about me, I let him hold me. I pushed the door closed and wrapped my arms around his waist, enjoying the comfort of home for just a moment. A few tears even leaked out again to stain his shirt a darker color.

He pulled back and framed my face with his hands, leaning down to look me over. "You okay?"

Taking a deep breath, I nodded and let him lead me to my couch. He held my hands as we sat beside each other.

"What are you doing here?" I asked, it finally hitting me how crazy it was for him to be at my door past ten on a Friday night when he should've been in Texas.

"I missed you." His answer easily slid off his tongue, like it was a fact of life, so obvious that he was confused why I needed to question it. "And after that message you sent me about missing me too, I had to come." I hadn't exactly said I missed him, but I didn't interrupt. "I wanted to surprise you. I came by but you weren't home, so I decided to have a coffee across the street and wait. I'd only gotten in a while ago, so I wasn't waiting long. Figured I'd try your door one more time before I headed to my hotel and called you."

"It's a nice surprise. I miss you too." He couldn't have come at a better time. I needed a piece of home and while he'd shocked me, I couldn't deny how good it felt to not be alone. To have the comfort of a friend when I was in so much doubt about my choices.

"I hate seeing you sad, Jules." His eyes looked over my face and a hand lifted to brush my cheek and push hair back behind my ear.

"Me too. Or I hate being sad." I laughed weakly as I rummaged through my mind on how to explain why I was such a mess. "It's just been a long week with work and stuff."

"I hate that you aren't close so I can comfort you. Don't you miss us? Our friendship?"

A small warning bell chimed in the back of my mind. Surely Hudson wouldn't have traveled all this way just to try and convince me to go back home. I remembered my conversation with my mom and proceeded with caution.

"Of course, I miss our friendship," I said, purposefully ignoring his "us" comment. "But distance doesn't have to mean we can't be friends."

"Do you have anyone here that can comfort you like me?" he argued.

I sat up straighter, feeling a little defensive. "I have Jo."

"Where is Jo now?" He lifted his hands wide and looked around my apartment as though Jolene would pop out from behind the couch. He leveled me with a look that I knew meant he was about to make his argument, but was trying to come off as pleading. I knew him so well. "Jules, you can come home. Be a scientist there. We can move closer to the city so you're not under your parents' thumb. I'll be there for you. It doesn't have to be the high-society life you hate."

For a moment, the plan he set out sounded more enticing than I anticipated. I would have the opportunity to keep working. To have a man I felt secure with. Still be close to my parents. It was all laid out before me, and I was tempted to agree to anything to help me feel better.

But then I remembered my family, the life. We could move closer into the city, but Hudson would still be working for my father. I'd still be required to go to gala functions, take on a charity. Then how much time would I have to give up at the lab until it was too much and I'd have to walk away? How much of myself would I have to sacrifice until there was nothing left?

I pulled my hands into my lap. "Hudson, I can't. I'm happy here."

"Happy?" he asked, incredulously. His coaxing tone shifting to frustration. "You don't look very happy, Juliana."

"It's just been a bad week," I said defensively.

He stared at me, jaw clenched, eyes scanning my face, thinking over his next plan of attack.

"Is it because of that man I saw fucking you earlier?"

I choked on my breath, my eyes growing wide with shock. "What?"

"Really? In an alley? Out in public?" His lips curled in disgust and I swallowed hard, unable to process anything. "Is this what you want to be? Is this why you want to be away, so you can sleep around?"

"Hudson." His name was barely air passing over my lips as I tried to regain my composure. But instead, I felt lightheaded, the tingling of frustration prickling up my spine.

"I love you, Juliana." His proclamation sounded angry and not at all sweet like an I love you should come out. "Enough to look past this last year and whatever else you've done. But you have to meet me half way."

He spoke as though he was doing me a favor for loving me. And it pissed me off. "I don't want to meet you anywhere, Hudson."

"No, you just want to meet a man in an alley to get fucked. And by someone who so obviously hurts you."

"That's enough." My tone was hard and in control. I couldn't believe all the things he was saying, and so cruelly. He was supposed to be my friend and right then he was being a dick. "My sex life is none of your business."

"Your 'sex life' is shameful. Shameful enough to need space to do it away from family. Is that the only reason you left?"

"Enough." I raised my voice, letting him know I was done allowing him to sit in *my* apartment and talk down to me. I was so sick and tired of people talking down to me. *Fuck him.* I stood, staring down at him with barely concealed anger. "I left because I didn't want to stay and become a *kept* woman, passed from my father to a husband chosen for me. I can be strong by making my own choices. I'm so sick and tired of explaining that to people." He opened his mouth to speak, but I held up my hand and kept going. "I may get hurt and make decisions you don't agree with, but they are *my* choices and *I* lived them. At least I'm living the way I wanted."

He stood with his jaw clenched, trying to regain his composure. "I'm just worried about you, Juliana."

I walked past him and opened my door. "Don't be. I'm fine all on my own."

I wouldn't meet his eyes as he walked out. We'd grown up together and as much as I hadn't seen the side of him he just unleashed on me, he'd seen my stubborn side enough to know I was done.

He walked out and I slammed the door behind him, feeling better than before he came. All that talk reminded me how strong I was. I may have been hurt then, but I knew I was strong enough to get past it. The soft pain hardened a little bit more, reminding me I was a bad-ass bitch all on my own.

Chapter Twenty-Four

Part of me wanted to wallow in my misery the whole weekend through, but I'd done that last weekend and I just wanted my family at that point. I wanted to laugh at their stories even if it hurt, because maybe for a moment in time, I'd forget the pain taking up residence inside me. I needed to remind myself that everything I needed was here in Cincinnati.

Jolene and I had had a girls' night and stuffed our faces with Cincinnati-style pizza and Grater's ice cream, which made me a little sad. I'd had Grater's for the first time with Shane, the same night I'd fallen in love with him. However, when Jo saw my frown, she insisted we make new memories to go with the glorious-ness that was Grater's. We'd danced with pints and spoons in our hands and passed out watching rom-coms.

When Sunday rolled around, I walked into King's late since the customary construction traffic seemed to have been even worse today. I opened the door with an energy I didn't possess, and a smile on my face, even if it was a little forced. Fake it until you make it, right? Luella and Evie greeted me with forced smiles of their own, and Jameson just stared from behind the bar. I stumbled over my feet a little, taking in their concerned faces. I fought off the furrowing of my brow and smiled even harder, refusing to let their worried expressions bring me down. I shrugged off my purse and walked to the table.

"Hey ladies." I said with fake happiness in my tone, but it faded off when, out of the corner of my eye, I saw Jack appear from the back hallway, head bent as he listened to Hudson.

Hudson.

Fucking Hudson.

My eyes widened and I clamped my jaw shut to prevent it from hitting the floor. Jack looked pissed, which pissed me off because I could only imagine what the hell Hudson was spewing to him.

Catching Hudson's eyes, I was met with a victorious glint. The jealous little weasel was using my family against me, and I wanted to make him choke on his balls. Fuck him. He didn't get to come here and mess with my life. I opened my mouth and raised my hand, preparing to stomp over and lay into him good when the door opened behind me.

Jack's concerned scowl morphed into a murderous glare, and I didn't need to turn to see who stood behind me. Jack's fists clenched as tight as his jaw, and he began taking long strides to the man behind me.

"You son of a bitch," Jack growled out the words.

Jameson stepped out from behind the bar and intercepted Jack, holding him back. "No fighting in my bar."

Jack didn't even acknowledge him as he strained against Jameson's arms. "You fucked my sister." He roared it so loud, I wouldn't be surprised if everyone on the block heard.

"Jack," I said. I didn't know what the hell I wanted. For him to shut up? For him to never ever say anything about me being fucked again? For Shane to leave? What the hell was he doing here, anyway? Did he want to torture me more?

I really just wanted to feel like I had control of the situation, of my life.

"Look man . . ." Shane started and his voice sent chills down my spine. I hated myself for feeling anything from his voice.

"In a fucking alley, like she's one of the random whores you screw around with."

Shane didn't even try to defend himself. "Jack, I'm sorry."

"Go, Juliana." Evie muttered beneath her breath at the table, but still loud enough to hear.

"Shut the fuck up, Evie." Jack didn't even look at her as he snapped his words.

"Watch your mouth, Jack," Jameson warned, his arm tightening around Jack more forcefully.

Jack was too far gone to acknowledge his mistake, too focused on Shane. "You're like my brother. I trusted you. Just so you could screw my baby sister."

"Enough," I shouted. I was done being talked about like a child who wasn't there. "I'm a big girl, Jack. I can make my own decisions, and you need to calm down."

"Calm down? He degraded you. Used you."

"Stop it!" The situation was spiraling downhill, faster than I could control it. I still hadn't turned to look at Shane, but I could feel him. And Jack's rage was another living being in the room, trying to break free of Jameson and unleash hell on Shane. "You're exaggerating, and you need to get it together," I said, pointing at him before turning my finger to Hudson, who was leaning against the wall like it was some free show. "And you're a fucking, conniving dick."

"Well that conniving dick—who was looking out for you— came to me after finding you crying last night. *Shane* is why you've been so depressed lately," Jack said. It wasn't a question. He was beyond any of my input. "So not only did he fuck you, but he hurt you by throwing you away. It's what he does."

"It's not what-" Shane tried to defend himself.

"It is. I've watched you since I've known you use one woman after the next."

"It's not like-"

"And now you've moved on to my sister."

"Jack, I-"

"I trusted you. You were my brother."

"I *am* your brother. It's not-"

"You *used* her like a-"

"I love her!" Shane roared.

The room fell silent at his proclamation. The words rattled around in my head and my heart beat too hard, unsure what to feel. My stomach churned as I tried to process it all. Evie and Luella gaped at each other. I blinked over and over trying to prevent the tears from burning the backs of my eyes.

I slowly turned, finally looking at Shane. He looked exhausted. Dark circles bruised under his bloodshot eyes. His shoulders dropped as his mouth opened and closed, searching for words.

"You *what?*" I whispered.

"I . . .I didn't mean . . .Shit, Juliana. I didn't-"

I stomped forward until I stood right in front of him, jaw clenched, shock and anger fueling the blood in my veins.

"What? You didn't *mean* it?" I jabbed him in the chest. "You just wanted to try and salvage your family with whatever means necessary?"

"No. Jules, I didn't-"

"Then why? Why?" I could barely form any other words. My throat was closing over the lump trying to escape.

His cheeks were red and he looked more unsure than I'd ever seen him. Stuttering over his words, starting sentence after sentence, but finishing none of them. Part of me wanted to let him off the hook, but my emotions raged so high after the stress of everything. The angry words thrown back and forth, Hudson coming to me Friday night, Hudson standing there after spilling my life to my brother. I was too pissed.

"I've missed you." His words were soft, spoken only to me and it was the first bit of hurt to break past the anger, bringing a tear with it. But the hurt just added fire to the anger and I lashed out.

"*Missed* me? Like you *missed* me Friday night? Missed my moans when you're inside me? My skin, my lips, my taste?" I ignored Jack's growl as I threw Shane's words back in his face from Friday.

"Juliana." He said my name like a plea, filled with hurt. "No."

"No? Then what is it about me that you *miss*?" I needed him to tell me he missed me as a human being, as someone who shared moments with him. Not just a body he missed fucking. I needed him to do more than stand before me, looking miserable. I needed words.

"I . . .I miss . . ." He looked around the room as he rubbed a hand over his hair to squeeze the back of his neck.

"You don't even know. You can't even say it." I wiped at the stray tears falling down my cheek and hardened my voice. "You don't love me. Someone who loved me wouldn't leave me feeling so miserable over and over. Reject my love again and again. They wouldn't say the things you've said to me, telling me I'm not worth the risk. You don't even know what love is."

I pushed past him and dodged to avoid his hand reaching out. Grabbing my purse, I ignored the scuffle of sound behind me. I ignored the sound of skin hitting skin as I tore open the door and made my escape.

Chapter Twenty-Five

Jolene and I each had a pint of Talenti in our laps, feet kicked up on the ottoman, a bottle of wine between us-no glasses needed, and stared at Ryan Reynold's sexy ass while we watched *Deadpool*. I'd walked in the door, my eyes dry but puffy and red, and Jo had given me a sad look that lasted all of two seconds, before heading to the kitchen for ice cream and spoons.

I plopped on the couch and when she brought an uncorked bottle of wine, I tipped it back with a few long pulls. Then I reached my hand out for mint chocolate chip and dug in. It was about seven scoops, two more chugs, and five minutes of the movie that I began spilling what had happened. Jolene respectively gave me a lot of "Fuck thats", "I'm sorrys," and "What a bunch a dicks," which made me love her even more.

Then *she'd* taken long pulls from the bottle. Which was how we ended up with a second bottle of wine, half of it gone, when the knock on the door came.

She turned to look at me with eyebrows raised. "We can pretend to not be home."

"*Deadpool* is kind of loud. Ryan Reynolds is giving away that we're home."

"What a sexy dick."

We giggled like two girls who'd drank two bottles of wine in less than an hour. When the knock came again, Jo was the one to stumble to the door. I didn't turn around, too scared to see who it was, and finished off the last of the wine.

"Are you the bearers of good or evil?" Jo asked in a dramatic voice that sounded slightly British. I laughed into my hand.

"I like to think I'm a little bit a both, but if I had to choose one, I'm pretty evil," Evie said.

"Ugh. Stop it." It sounded like Luella hit Evie. "We're here to see Jules. See how she is."

"Come on in," I called from the couch.

Evie and Lu came to sit on the other two chairs in the living room and took in the empty wine bottles and ice cream.

"Guys want some wine?" Jo came back holding another bottle of wine. "We're keeping it classy with no glasses, so I hope you don't mind germs," she said before taking a drink.

"These are my kind of people," Evie said with a grin as she reached for the bottle.

Luella shook her head when Evie offered her some, then looked at me. "How are you?"

"Kind of shitty. Kind of drunk."

She gave me a sympathetic look. "If it makes you feel better, we calmed Jack down a little. Evie bringing up how he was banging me, Jameson's little sister, without being punched made him look at it in a different light. Kind of."

"Ugh. I don't care about stupid Jack and his hissy fit." I threw my hands up and fell back on the cushion. Biting my lip, I weighed the pros and cons of the next question. "Shane?"

"He's . . .Okay. I guess."

"He left after your brother clocked him," Evie said without softening the blow before taking another swig of wine. Lu elbowed her and she shrugged. "What? It's what happened."

"He was just shocked. You're his baby sister."

"I'm not a baby."

"In his eyes, you are."

"I mean, I think we all were a little shocked by you and Shane's crazy sex," Evie said, passing the bottle to me.

I took a drink and scoffed, passing the wine to Jo. "How were *you* shocked by this," I asked Evie, accusation coloring my tone.

She raised one eyebrow. "Excuse me?"

"This is all your fault. You pushed me at him. You made me love him." I threw the words at her with a slur, letting myself unleash some blame onto someone else's shoulders. Wrong or not, it was happening. "Now I'm in this mess because of your encouragement."

"Jules," Jo said softly, placing a hand on my shoulder.

"No," Evie said, holding up her hand, her narrowed eyes trained on me. "First things first." She pointed her finger in my direction. "You need to own up to your choices." I opened my mouth to defend myself. "Period. Now, I'm not going to patronize you like your brother, or say you're too young, because I can see you have your shit together. But having your shit together does not give you experience. Which is why I'm going to let that misplaced pissiness slide."

I sulked back against the couch. Evie had a way with words that made you feel good about yourself while still having the upper hand. I knew I was wrong for laying any blame at her feet. I just needed to share the heaviness that weighed on me.

"How many relationships have you been in? How many men have you been with? Or better yet, how many men have you *really* wanted?"

"I dated Hudson, but it was more out of convenience and expectation. There was also a random one-night stand."

"Anyone you truly chased? Someone you hardcore went after? Other than Shane."

I shook my head, trying to figure out where she was going, but the wine made it hard. "Not really."

"See," she said with excitement, like her point was already made. When I just sat and stared at her in confusion she went on to explain. "You didn't have experience to know that you would have gone after Shane even without my alleged permission. Nothing was stopping that."

She reached across me and grabbed the wine bottle, finishing it off. I let her words sink in. Would I have gotten together with Shane without a shove from Evie? Probably. I mean, I did in Jamaica, and I'd been dying for a second chance ever since.

Rolling my eyes, I knew she was right. I needed to take responsibility for my choices, even if they did suck and I hated the way they made me feel.

"What do I do now?" I asked, almost whining.

"He said he loved you," Lu said, reminding me like I didn't have the words on repeat, haunting me.

"He didn't mean it. We fucked, but he never said anything about wanting more. That was all me and my imagination conjuring more."

"Then why would he say it?" Jo asked, returning from the kitchen with another bottle of wine.

I snagged it from her hand and drank.

"I don't know. Maybe to sound better in front of Jack? That's what he said when I told him I loved him. That he couldn't lose Jack as a brother. That I wasn't 'worth it'. Maybe if Jack believed he loved me, he'd forgive him."

"You said you loved him and he turned you down? Then comes in and shouts it out to everyone? Oh *hell* no." Evie shook her head and pursed her lips.

"Yeah, I mean Jack is great, and I could see why he'd want to keep that friendship. But you're a woman that will be his companion," Luella said. "I mean, you have a vagina . . .that he can have sex with."

"Here, here for vaginas." Evie lifted the bottle and drank. Even Lu snagged it from her and took a sip.

We all fell into a fit of drunken giggles. But once that bottle was gone and Jo informed us we had no more, we got back to the heart of the issue.

"So, what do you want to do?" Evie asked.

"Not hurt anymore."

"That's up to you. You can believe him and go to him. Or you move on."

"How?"

"I don't know how to help you believe him or not, but if you want to move on, you make your decision and stick to it. Remove yourself from him and the temptation, because nothing is harder than facing him and trying to give him up."

"Trust her, she would know. She failed that way with James-on," Lu joked, elbowing Evie.

"You have to be sure and strong in your choice. Don't waffle back and forth. Like I said, you have your shit together. So be the strong independent woman who moved here to support herself without any help. You don't need anyone. You're Juliana Mac-Cabe, badass bitch of the Midwest."

Her hiccup at the end of her speech kind of dimmed it, but it still lit a fire in me. I *was* badass bitch of the Midwest. I didn't need his love to feel good. I didn't need his protection. I didn't need anything but these awesome ladies here.

My mind began spinning with what I wanted to do to pull away from him, because as much as my heart was dying to believe him, I couldn't be foolish anymore. I couldn't let my imagination run free conjuring pictures of a happily ever after. He knew my body, but he didn't know me well enough to love me. I had to face facts.

"I'll have to pull out of the forensic position at the station."

"You only had two weeks left anyways. Dr. Voet will let you do that. He'd let you do anything after Friday's date."

Both Evie and Lu looked at me with eyebrows in their hair lines. "Whaaa?"

I waved off their shocked interest. "The date didn't go as well as planned. He's great, but I just wasn't ready."

"Sorry, babe. This is growing up and unfortunately there are no answers," Evie said.

"It kind of sucks," Lu added.

Jolene fell back onto the couch beside me and we all stared up at the ceiling. "Life is such a bitch."

True, but starting tomorrow, I was going to make life *my* bitch.

Chapter Twenty-Six

"When are you going to ask Dr. Voet about not going back to the station?" Jolene asked me from the other side of the elevator.

I rubbed my tired eyes. "I don't know. It's only two more weeks. Maybe I can just avoid Shane."

She didn't respond, just gave me a condescending stare.

"What?"

"How many times has he called?"

Shane had called no less than seven times since yesterday when I left King's. Jolene had hidden my phone from me last night, so by the time I'd seen them on my screen the next morning, I ignored them all and refused to listen to the messages. I'd made my decision last night. I needed to stick to it.

"Ugh!" I rolled my eyes at her as we got off the elevator. "I'll talk to Calvin today," I said, caving to her point.

We turned to head back to our lab from lunch. Ready to finish the last half of the day. When we made the final turn to our hallway, we heard Dr. Stahl yelling from Dr. Voet's office.

"Oh, yay," Jo said. "More yelling. As though there wasn't enough from this morning."

Dr. Stahl had been in a shit mood today. More so than other days. Stomping into the room, letting doors slam against walls before slamming closed. Barking short, clipped orders at us from his office, not even deigning us worthy of talking to like we were respectable humans.

"This is the third time she's signed off on deliveries where lab products have gone missing. *Three times.* How much longer are we going to let this continue?"

Jo looked at me with wide eyes and I sighed in dread. I had no idea what was going on with the missing supplies, but every day we didn't know, I felt my job slipping further and further from my grasp. Wouldn't that be the icing on the cake?

"The situation is being handled." Dr. Voet's voice rumbled low and calm, the complete opposite of Dr. Stahl's.

"What the hell does that mean? It's *my* lab. I should be informed of how it's being handled."

"It's officially the college's lab and the college's equipment and materials."

"This is bullshit. A pretty face and a set of breasts are distracting you from the obvious."

"That's enough, Andrei." For the first time, Dr. Voet raised his voice.

I closed my eyes, feeling shame for something I had no control over. Dr. Stahl was a misogynistic dick, and I had nothing to feel embarrassed about.

After a long silence, Dr. Stahl spoke softer than before, but with no less frustration. "I expect this to be taken care of."

Jo and I didn't have time to move along and pretend we hadn't heard every bit of that argument when Dr. Stahl came storming out, lab coat fanning behind him like a villain's cape. He walked through the second door and stopped when he saw us standing wide-eyed across the hall.

It was the first time we'd seen him all morning since he'd holed himself up in his office. Jo had had to teach his first two classes impromptu because of his absence. He looked haggard. Like he hadn't been sleeping or eating. His dark hair looked greasy and in disarray, either from not combing it or running his hands through it. His dark eyes sunk a little deeper and stood out more with the circles rimming his eyes.

"Get back to work," he ordered.

I looked through the door to see Dr. Voet standing behind him in the doorway, watching me. I met his eyes for a moment, but looked away, not quite ready to stay and make my request.

"Now!" Dr. Stahl shouted, making Jo and I scurry down the hall.

The afternoon passed ridiculously slowly, dragging out the time, almost taunting me to go see Calvin and plead my case to not go back to the police station. Every time I got a break in a procedure, Jo would sing-song that now was as good a time as any. I ignored her and moved on to the next procedure.

Maybe a little after five, with my eyes glued to the microscope, Jo's shocked voice said, "What is he doing here?"

I looked up to find Dr. Voet, a few police officers, and Shane and his partner walking through the door to our lab. Shane stood broader than them all. He almost seemed too big for the room as he walked toward Dr. Stahl's office but his blue eyes remained on me, holding me captive for too long. I cringed seeing the bruise on his cheek that came from Jack's punch.

"I don't know."

My heart hammered in my chest and tingles radiated throughout my body until my skin seemed to buzz with shock. I hadn't been prepared to see him so soon. I had decided to block him out and there he was in my space. In *my* lab. He wasn't allowed in there.

A scuffle came from Dr. Stahl's office and muffled shouts had Jo and I staring, frozen in our spot. Two officers had one of Dr. Stahl's arms firmly gripped in a hand each, with his wrists cuffed together behind his back.

"Andrei Stahl, you are under arrest for stealing property from the University of Cincinnati and distributing said property to known drug manufacturers."

"Holy shit," Jo breathed beside me.

"Fuck you," Dr. Stahl spat at Dr. Voet. "I'm sick and tired of being beholden to this cheap American college." He turned his attention on us, pure fire burning in his eyes. "Women shouldn't be allowed in a lab. These conditions are unforgivable for someone as successful as I am."

The officers returned to reading him his rights as they walked him out of the room. After he'd disappeared through the doors, I turned to Jo. I was sure her slacked jaw and wide-eyes mirrored my own.

"What the fuck?"

Jo and I were still staring at each other, looking like we were both on the verge of uncomfortable laughter, when Shane walked over.

"Are you okay?"

His deep voice stroked my skin, urging me to turn and look at him. I didn't want to. But, at the same time, I really did. It was the fact that I was dying to turn and let my eyes devour him that made me clamp my jaw shut and turn to look at him with as much fire as I could muster.

"What are you doing here?"

"Arresting him."

"Don't you work on arresting murderers?"

He looked a little nervous and brought his hand up to rub across his neck before answering. "Uh, sometimes it intertwines with drugs." His hand moved up through his hair and his partner Reese walked up behind him. "I just wanted to be here for you. Make sure you're okay."

"Yeah, you should have seen this guy's face when he saw your name on the police report and realized it was where you worked. I thought he was going to blow an artery."

"Reese." Shane's voice rang low and warning.

"Said we had to be here to protect MacCabe's little sister and make sure you're okay. Lucky girl to have so many people watching out for you."

MacCabe's little sister.

"I just wanted to make sure you were safe from any fallout."

All I heard from Reese's retelling was *MacCabe's little sister. Protect her.* I was so sick and tired of having to say it over and over again.

"I don't need protection, Shane. I don't need to be rescued."

"I know that."

"Do you?" I asked, narrowing my eyes at him. "I thought you did. I thought you treated me as an equal when we were together. But here you are." I looked him up and down. "Protecting Mac-Cabe's little sister. Treating me as a child who can't stand on her own two feet."

"You're with Jack MacCabe's little sister? You got a death wish, man?" Reese asked.

"Shut up, Reese," Shane growled at him. He took a deep breath and stepped closer to me, trying to talk lower so only I could hear. "I miss you."

"We've already had this conversation, and yet you just don't get it. You left me twice. *Twice.*" I held up two fingers to make my point, because words weren't seeming to work. "And despite all my proclamations to every man around me that *I'm fine* on my own, they are continually ignored, because *apparently* I don't know better for myself."

"I made a mistake." He held out his hands in supplication, looking defeated. "You were right. I was scared of what you made me feel."

His words thumped against the wall I'd built around myself

in the last thirty-six hours. I stared into his eyes and a part of me wanted to. I really, *really* wanted to believe him.

But then I remember all the times he called me a child. I remembered the time he told me I was a nice fuck, but a mistake. I remembered the time I told him I loved him and practically begged him to love me back, and he turned me away. I remembered when he told me I wasn't worth it. I saw how he treated me just like Jack, my father, and Hudson; always assuming they knew what was best for me, despite my direct wishes.

"You need to leave." I hated the slight waver in my voice. "Go take in your criminal."

"Jules, let me help."

"I don't need your help." My raised voice drew attention from outside as Dr. Voet walked in. "I'm fine on my own."

"Everything okay in here?" Dr. Voet asked.

I stared at Shane as he breathed heavily, seeming to weigh his options. Reese rested a palm on his shoulder as though letting him know it was time to go.

"Yeah," Shane said. "Just asking some questions. We'll be heading out now."

And he turned to walk away, staring at Dr. Voet as he walked past.

"You okay?" Dr. Voet asked me, his hands coming to rest on my shoulders."

I swallowed hard and nodded, even though I felt far from okay. Especially when I met Shane's hollow eyes as he walked out the door.

Was I making a mistake?

Chapter Twenty-Seven

The first gift arrived on Tuesday. It was a small gift bag that the department secretary placed on my desk. When I asked who it was from, she shrugged and said a student delivered it. I removed the tissue paper and pulled out a . . .

Lunchable? A pizza lunchable.

"Who the hell gift wraps a pizza lunchable?" Jolene asked. "That's a shitty gift."

I looked in the bag to see if there was more and saw a piece of paper stuck to the bottom that said 'read me.' Of course, curiosity had me unfolding it, because Jo was right, who the hell sent a lunchable as a gift.

Juliana,

A pizza lunchable because it already comes apart and I know how much you enjoy your pizza in pieces. I miss sitting across from you at Sunday brunch, and watching you eat the toppings, then the cheese, and finally the crust. You never noticed me watching, but I always was. I can't remember a time when my eyes weren't drawn to you.

I miss you,
Shane

P.S. My favorite pizza toppings are meat. All of them. I figured I'd share since I know you like green peppers, onions, mushrooms, and sausage. I also know you only like mushrooms on pizza. No other way.

I wanted to roll my eyes and be unaffected, but it was too soon, and I was too close to crying. I was about to toss it, but Jo said she'd eat it. I'd stared at the cheap yellow plastic with crappy pizza crust and sauce behind it, and felt possessive over it. It was mine.

But I made sure not to enjoy it.

⟶

Wednesday, I got a flat box, wrapped in simple blue paper. When the secretary passed it to me, I carefully held it like I would a bomb. Jolene rolled over and bounced in her seat to see what the next gift would be.

Swallowing hard, I began tearing through the paper, revealing a white clothing box. Opening that, I saw a shirt peeking out of tissue paper.

Let's cuddle and talk about science.

I didn't want to laugh at how perfect it was. I didn't want to feel my eyes burning for a third day in a row. I wanted to be indifferent.

Setting the shirt aside, I saw another piece of paper at the bottom of the box. Carefully, I unfolded it and began reading.

Juliana,

I love the shirts you wear. Every time I saw you, I looked forward to what they would say because they always made me laugh. I miss seeing the way they fit you perfectly, outlining the perfect curve of your breasts. Because, yes, I miss all of you. Every part.

Forgive me,

Shane

P.S. I collect CPD shirts. Mainly because they're free, but also because I love the station and the shirts are always soft.

My heart raced and my lungs struggled to keep up. Losing the battle, I wiped a lone tear off my cheek and placed the shirt back in the box. Jo was kind enough to not point it out and we got back to work.

I realized what he was doing. Showing me how much he knew me, and I couldn't deny enjoying the attention, but it hurt so much because I'd made my decision. Why hadn't all this effort come before? Why did I have to be crushed for him to decide he cared?

My nerves tingled with both excitement and dread over what the next day would hold.

❧

Thursday, a Christmas Cookie-scented Yankee Candle was sitting in a bag, with a lighter that said, "Baby you light up my world." Another note was stuck to the bottom and my hand trembled a little when I opened it.

Juliana,

I know you love citrus and vanilla candles. Really any baked good-scented candle. But I know that Christmas Cookie is your favorite. It's also ridiculously hard to find in the spring. My days are a lot darker without your smile.

I miss you,

Shane

P.S. My favorite scent is vanilla on your skin.

I laid the note on my bench and brought the candle to my nose to smell, and I smiled.

❧

I waited all day Friday. Every time the door opened my head shot up and my heart beat in double-time. But every person that walked through the door came with empty hands. No gift showed up that day and as the minutes ticked by, I learned how much they were breaking down my walls to be so disappointed with the mere possibility he'd officially given up on me.

My insides were a juxtaposition of hope for more and determination to stay strong against giving in. I was scared as to which would win out.

Dr. Voet had caught me on my way out, and with a hopeful but hesitant expression, asked me if I wanted to grab some dinner. I think he knew the answer before I even gave him a regretful smile. He'd been understanding and said he'd still love my company in the mornings for non-coffee. Jolene walked up beside us and invited herself to that party saying she'd bring the creamer next Monday.

I hadn't expected anything over the weekend, assuming Shane had given up after not hearing from me. So, when I opened the door to a courier asking me to sign for a package, I couldn't stop the excited smile that stretched my cheeks. I tore open the padded manila envelope and greeting cards slipped out.

Juliana,

Five blank cards for you to keep for whatever it is that you collect them for. I love it about you. I love that you have a drawer dedicated to cards that make you happy. I thought of you with every one I looked at, trying to imagine the sound of your sweet laugh as though you were there with me.

I love you,

Shane

P.S. I'm sorry I missed yesterday. Work was rough and long. I missed not having you to hold me and run your fingers through my hair when the day is hard. Even when I was scared of my feelings for you, I couldn't stay away no matter how much I tried. Every night I'd come to you for comfort and you never turned me away. I was unworthy of it, but I'm selfish and miss it all the same.

I began reading through each card, laughing at them all. Wishing I had been there with him to go through the cards and listen to his deep rumble when he laughed too.

"I wanted to send you something sexy, but the postman told me to get out of the box."

"You must have a p-value of at least 0.05 because I fail to reject you."

"I can't believe how much I'm not sick of you."

"Roses are red, but sometimes their thorny. When you're not with me, I get sorta . . . Corny."

"I just want you to be happy (and naked) but mostly happy."

Tears mixed with my laughter and for the first time, I really wanted to pick up my phone and call or text him. But I didn't know how. Where did it leave us? Did he still think of me as Jack's little sister, in need of protection? As someone who wasn't an equal?

I ran my fingers over his *I love you*, and the walls I'd erected against him cracked a little more. Maybe he *did* know me. Maybe he did love me.

I just didn't know what to do with it yet.

Sunday, I opened my door to a mug that read "Well Shit", with hot chocolate stuffed inside. A note fell out from between the two packets when I pulled them out.

Juliana,

I love your love for mugs. Even when you don't drink hot coffee. I figured maybe some hot chocolate would make them feel more useful.

I still miss you,

Shane

P.S. I collect pictures of Cincinnati, because you were right, I do love the city.

꙰

Monday, a small velvet box showed up at work and I cracked it open slowly. A silver bangle bracelet shined against deep blue velvet. I pulled it out and read the inscription. *She believed she could, so she did.*

Juliana,

You are stronger than most men. Don't let anyone make you feel less than. Even me.

I believe in you,

Shane

Biting my lip, I slipped the cool metal on my wrist, already feeling stronger with the words.

꙰

Nothing came on Tuesday and I began to give up on Wednesday when a knock on the door came. A courier with another package.

I pulled out a CD with a handwritten title "All the things I didn't say." Jo put it in for me. With "Can't Help Falling in Love" by Ingrid Michaelson playing in the background, I unfolded the note.

Juliana,

I love you. I'm so sorry I was stupid and didn't say it when you needed to hear it. You're right, I was scared. I know I told you a little about my time in the foster system, and it wasn't a horror story, but it wasn't anything great either.

I'd moved around so much and I never got to know anyone enough to love them, or have them love me. There was actually one family I'd stayed with for two years when I was twelve. After being bounced around for two years, I'd thought that was it. I loved the mom and dad and two brothers. For the first time since I'd lost my mom, I truly felt like I was home.

But the dad got a job overseas and I was put back into the system. After that, I'd hardened myself, never getting close to any family. As soon as I turned eighteen, I focused on me and my future, throwing myself into work. I know it's no excuse, but for over twenty years, my heart remained frozen there. Until you. You broke through.

I miss everything about you,

Shane

Jo held me as I cried for him. For how alone he must have felt. For how much shit he was dealt in life. I wanted him there so I could sit on his lap and hold him to me. I wanted so much, but I didn't know how to go about it.

I opened my messages and typed out no less then twenty-two before I ended up just sending "Hi." I sat, staring at the glowing screen hoping the three dots would pop up saying he was responding back, but nothing came. Eventually, sleep claimed me and I woke up gripping my phone to my chest.

When I pushed the home button, I saw his reply. "Hi." So simple, but a start. It was something. I stared at my phone until it was time to leave for work, still trying to come up with another message, but it never came. So, I closed my phone and went to work instead.

No gift came that day, and as much as I wanted to write it off to maybe another busy day at work, doubts began eating at me.

Before, when I shut him out, I was cold. Now? Now I was running over every detail that led me to that point. With every good memory, a bad one bled into it. My insecurities ate at me late into the night whispering in my head how I wasn't worth it.

"What are you waiting for?" Jo asked on Thursday after seeing how depressed I got when another day went without a package. She asked the same question that had rattled through my brain for days.

"I don't know," I whispered. Swallowing, I turned to look at her. "Maybe I'm not worth it."

"Hush. Of course, you are. You're amazing. Just call him."

"It's so easy, isn't it? And yet, every time I pick up the phone, I freeze with doubt."

"Jules."

"I'm an idiot. And the longer I let this go on, the worse it gets and yet I can't do anything. I don't know what's wrong with me."

She didn't say anything, just let me try to process my thoughts.

"I mean, what if I call him and we're together and he loves me and I love him, and it doesn't work out? What happens then? Do I just become another person who abandons him? Who hurts him? I pushed so hard and what if I ruin it?"

"You never know until you try."

"Thanks, Yoda."

"I never took you for a little baby-bitch."

"I'm not."

"Then stop acting like one."

Chapter Twenty-Eight

Each day that passed without another gift, without a text, I was sure he'd given up on me. Maybe he should have. I honestly didn't know anymore. I'd talked myself in so many circles, weighing so many pros and cons—some that didn't even exist outside of my own imagination—that I was frozen in doubt, mixed with a yearning I could barely stand.

When a gift came in to the lab on Friday, I set it aside without opening it. I couldn't at work. And maybe Jo was right, I was acting like a baby-bitch. But for a few more hours, I immersed myself in work and tried not to think about anything outside of the lab. I had control over my procedure, running it step-by-step, like I'd always known. I had no control over the flat gift currently leaning against my desk.

I thought Jo was going to blow an artery when I told her I was going to wait until we got home. She became like a little child on Christmas day with the way she badgered me.

"Can we open it now? How about now? Now?"

When we got home, later than usual, she stared me down.

"Open the damn gift."

"Can I use the bathroom first?"

"No. You went before we left, so stop stalling or I'm going to get you a shirt with a cat on it. Make you wear it around so everyone knows what a pussy you are."

I glowered at her, but snatched up the gift and sat on the couch. She plopped down beside me and bounced like a child.

I opened it slowly, revealing a wide wooden picture frame holding a black and white photo. It was of the street sign on the corner of 5th and Vine.

"What the hell is that?"

Shrugging, I flipped the frame over to find a folded piece of paper taped to the back.

Juliana,

This is the spot I fell in love with you. I didn't know it then. But I watched you laugh and twirl to the fading salsa music, not caring who saw or what they thought. Watching you felt like a punch to the chest. I couldn't breathe. It felt like my heart was growing too big as it beat faster and faster, crushing my lungs.

You halted your dancing to look up at me and it all stopped. I leaned down to kiss you, trying to swallow up some of your joy. I was desperate for you that night. I was desperate to be deeper inside you, cover every inch of your body, leave my mark on you. I'd never wanted to be a part of someone as much as I wanted to be a part of you.

And it scared the shit out of me.

I'm sorry I pulled away.

I'm sorry I fought so hard.

But right there on that street corner, it changed everything. I wanted you to know, and have a memento of when you broke through my walls. I wanted you to know the exact moment you changed my life.

This will be the last letter. Not because I'm not sleeping with my phone gripped in my hand. Not because I'm not hoping you show up at my door. But because I want to show you how much I respect the decisions you make for yourself. And if space is what you need, then I hear you. I will always be here.

I love you,

Shane

"So help me god, if you don't call him, I'm going to track him down and hump him against his will. If you're too scared, then I will happily be his rebound."

I swallowed the lump in my throat and turned to narrow my eyes at her.

"Don't look at me like that. You don't get to claim him forever if you don't go get him."

"I know that."

"Then go fucking get him."

"I've waited two weeks," I argued.

"Shut up."

"Jolene."

"I said shut your face. No more excuses. No more doubt. If that giant, ice-box of a man can write that, then you will shove your doubts aside and prance your happy ass over to him."

Taking a deep breath, I thought of what to do next. Jo was right. I needed to go to him.

"Tomorrow."

"What? No, you will go right now."

"No." I stood firm in my decision. "I need a plan and I want to return the favor. I want to get him something. He's spent so much time sending me things to let me know how much he cares. I just . . .I just want to do something in return."

"I think your vagina will suffice."

"It's not about the sex. The fact that he assumed it was, is what got us here in the first place."

"Fine." She rolled her eyes before pointing at me. "But you *will* go see him tomorrow, even if I have to drag you kicking and screaming."

"Yes, mother."

"Good. Now get some sleep. You look like hell and you have a man to go claim tomorrow."

"You're too kind to me," I deadpanned.

Jo waved as she headed to her bedroom. I grabbed a shower and headed to bed. I did look like hell from the lack of sleep I'd had all week. I needed all the beauty sleep I could get tonight.

But it never came.

I stared at the ceiling, letting the memories of Shane and I roll through my brain. I remembered every gift he'd sent. His smile, his laugh, the feel of his calloused hands on my skin. The feel of his full lips pressed to mine.

I imagined showing up tomorrow and him not being there. Or him being there and mad that I'd waited so long to come to him.

I imagined him opening the door and smiling, pulling me into a hug and holding me tighter than ever. I imagined laying in his arms as the sun rose in the morning. I didn't want to wake up one more day without knowing he was mine.

Fuck doubts.

Fuck the fear.

Fuck all the angry words we'd thrown at each other.

I rolled over to look at my clock and saw it was half past one. So late. Too late.

I didn't care. The idea came to me of what I wanted to give him and once it was there, I needed to implement my plan immediately.

I took a picture of my rumpled bed with my phone. Not the greatest photography, but it'd work. I loaded it to my computer, added some fancy filter, made it black and white, and printed it off.

Then I looked around my room, landing on an old family picture in a frame. Prying it open, I set the photo aside and placed the picture of my bed inside. Then I grabbed one of the cards he'd sent me, and wrote my own note in it. Licking the envelope, feeling lighter with each step I took toward him, I spotted the shirt he'd gotten me laying on my dresser.

I quickly stripped out of my sleep shirt, skipped a bra, and pulled on the shirt he'd given me. I looked in the mirror and remembered the last time I'd gone to see him on a whim. It's what had started all of this. I nodded at the confident woman, armed with a photo and a card, and made my way to my car.

Adrenaline coursed through me as I tightly gripped Betsy's wheel. The street lamps passed one by one, each marking the shrinking distance between me and the man I was going to claim as mine.

The streets were mostly empty as the clock got closer to two. My mind took off, trying to imagine all the outcomes of the night, but I refused to let them form, solely focusing on the one that started tonight's journey.

By the time I'd reached his building, my hands were sweaty from how tightly they gripped the leather steering wheel. My heart hammered in my chest, and my legs trembled with each step I took closer to him.

My head buzzing with excitement, I lifted my fist to knock on the door. Ready to stand there all night if need be. But it only took two knocks, and by the time I'd lifted my hand for a third, I'd already heard the shuffle of feet approaching the door.

I was hit with a sense of déjà-vu when my future opened the door with low slung sweats hanging precariously on his hips. One word slipped past his lips and sank into me.

"Juliana."

Chapter Twenty-Nine

"Hey."

He looked me over like I was mirage. Like I'd disappear at any moment. "Hi."

I laughed. "Look at us, just filled with all kinds of things to say."

One side of his mouth quirked up, and he stepped to the side. "Come on in."

I had to duck my head to smile, because he didn't seem at all concerned that I showed up at his place at two in the morning. He treated it like it was a normal social call and couldn't be happier to see me.

"I got your gifts," I said, tugging at the bottom of my shirt, to showcase the words.

"Good." He ran his hand over his head and gripped the back of his neck. "I uh . . .Hoped you didn't just throw them in the trash."

When he looked down at me with his icy-blue eyes, I saw the hope and fear swirling in them. I wondered what he saw in mine. Fear, hope, love, fear.

"I wanted to bring you something too." Holding the wrapped frame, I watched his large hand grip it and my heart pounded a million pumps per minute. It raced with so many emotions, all of them fighting for supremacy, making my body tremble as they all fired off inside me.

He motioned for me to follow him to the couch where we sat. He pulled off the paper and stared at the picture, swallowing, but not looking up at me. Did he get the importance?

"This was where I fell in love with you. In my bed that night you took me home and made love to me. I wanted you to have a memento of the moment you changed my life, too."

"Juliana . . .," he whispered, his mouth opening and closing. I couldn't read his eyes, but the fact that he wasn't smiling at me with adoring love, pulling me into his arms and never letting me go, made me rush to get it all out *just* in case he'd changed his mind sometime today.

"I get your fears. I get that you finally found a brother in Jack. I get that you're scared of losing that again."

He closed his eyes and clenched his jaw. "Do you pity me now that you know my story?"

"I could never pity you." I reached out and rested my hand on his. He turned his palm up into mine, holding onto me tight. A flicker of hope ignited in me. I needed him to know I respected and loved how open he was with me. I wanted him to know he wasn't alone in his fears.

"My fears are of always being thought of as a little girl. That I'd always be thought of as weak and unable to stand alone. I'm scared of never knowing my true potential if the people in my life hold me in a tiny bubble against my will."

He set the photo aside and grabbed my other hand, scooting closer to me. "I'm sorry for all the times I called you a child. I did it to keep distance between us. For months, I thought too much about the woman who snuck into my room in Jamaica. And I knew that I needed to remove temptation from myself. That, and I didn't want to just fuck you, and ruin the relationship with someone I called family for the first time in a long time."

I licked my lips, pulling his eyes to my mouth. I wanted him to kiss me. Instead, he scooted closer, our legs brushing, and lifted a hand to my cheek, running his thumb along my wet lips with a groan. Closing his eyes, he took a deep breath and I struggled to remain looking at his face when his abs rippled on the exhale. But he held my gaze again and the way his lips tipped on one side, kept my attention.

"It was one of the only times I'd underestimated you. Showing up at my door in that lingerie, forcing me to see you. And damn I couldn't have looked away even if I was on fire."

I bit my lips between my teeth and looked down, trying to hide how happy his words made me.

"One of the times?" I asked, picking up on that part.

His eyes turned serious again. "I underestimated how much I would fall for you. I underestimated your ability to break my walls down."

"I want to say I'm sorry, but I'm not. You were the first man to not treat me like a child who couldn't make decisions on her own. And even though you called me Mini MacCabe, you never looked at me like you saw my brother."

His nose scrunched up. "Fuck no, I didn't."

We both laughed and it felt amazing to hear the sound mixed together again. He waited until my eyes met his again and I couldn't look away from the fire starting to burn there.

"I'm not sorry for loving you. You scare the shit out of me. But I'm not sorry for falling in love with you."

I swallowed hard against the knot in my throat, but his words made my chest feel like it was filled with too much of everything.

"I love you, Juliana. I love how strong you are, how quirky you are, how smart you are. I love it all. I want you to be my family. And if Jack can't get over it, then that sucks, but you are worth it."

My chest shook with the first cry. Tears fell down my cheeks and he moved both palms to cup them and wiped the wetness away. He held his forehead to mine and whispered over and over, "Don't cry. Please don't cry. I love you. Please don't cry." I wrapped my arms around his shoulders and felt along the strong muscles I'd missed so much. His large body beneath my smaller hands, all of it so much more than I ever thought I'd feel again.

We were going to do this and I almost giggled through my tears with how happy the realization made me. Taking a deep breath, I sat back and wiped at my cheeks.

"Right here, right now. Let's make a pact. I will understand that you are a stubborn old man with a busy, dangerous job. But I promise, that I will be your family." Swallowing hard, I pushed on to give him my word, no matter how much the idea hurt me. "And if it doesn't work out, I will *still* be your family."

A sheen slipped over his eyes, making them seem brighter than before. He cleared his throat and it moved me that such a large, strong, island of a man could show so much emotion just from me telling him I'd always be his family.

He went to open his mouth and I held up my hand, needing to say one more thing. "Unless you cheat on me or you're a giant dick-hole. Then I will fuck up your world."

He chuckled and I held out my hand, wanting to shake on it. He slipped his long fingers along mine and cradled my palm, just holding my hand, not shaking it yet.

"I will respect that you are a woman who is independent and loves fiercely. I will understand that you are stubborn and that I will have to earn the right to protect you." I opened my lips, but his free hand covered them. "Not because I think you need it, but because I love you."

Smiling, I nodded and we finally shook on it.

It didn't last long before he tugged me into him and *finally* pressed his lips to mine. The kiss started slow, mimicking all the promises we'd made to each other. Slow enough to relearn the curve of each other's lips, the way the other tasted.

However, like all the other times we'd touched, our sparks exploded and lit a fire within us, and soon we were pushing our tongues deeper, trying to get closer to the other. Our hands searched and pulled and tugged. Our breaths picked up and matched our frantic movements.

Shane's hands moved to my bottom and tugged me across his lap to straddle him. His lips worked down my neck, sending chills over my body, as his hands worked under my shirt. They skated past my belly until they reached the curve of my breasts.

He growled when he discovered I hadn't worn a bra.

"Fuck, I love you."

He cradled my breasts in his hands and wrapped his mouth around a tip over the shirt, sucking hard, pulling moan after moan from my throat. I ground my core over his growing erection, desperate to feel more through my thin leggings. He nipped at me with his teeth before pulling back and whipping my shirt over my head, tossing it across the room.

I curved my body around his head as he latched on to my nipple and flicked his tongue back and forth, torturing me. Scraping my hands up his back, I gripped his short hair and tugged his head back, giving myself access to his lips.

Lifting up on my knees, I reached my hand between us, groping for his dick. He groaned when my fingers brushed the head over his thick sweatpants, but I wanted more. I wanted all of him. My other hand joined the first, and did their best to tug the material as far as it could go. He got the hint and lifted his hips to help me pull the material past his ass. His thick cock stood proud along his stomach, his heavy balls resting over the waistband of his pants.

"Oh, god," I breathed, pulling back to fall to the floor on my knees, immediately dragging my tongue up the sensitive back of his penis, just to suck on the head.

I teased and sucked and licked, taking him as deep as I could go, then going further, gagging on him. Each time, a moan would rip from his chest. I massaged his balls, rolling them in my hands, pressing my fingers to the skin behind them.

But I didn't want him to come in my mouth. I needed to feel him inside me, so I pulled off with a pop and stood between his spread legs.

Holding his stare, I turned, peeking over my shoulder as my thumbs slipped into the waistband of my leggings and I began to tug them down. I kept my legs straight the whole time, letting him see every inch of me as I bent over to get my pants completely off. When I turned, he'd already worked his pants off and grabbed a condom from the side table drawer. He leaned forward and gripped my hips, jerking me harshly to him, until I fell, supporting myself on the back of the couch.

"Ride me, little girl. Fuck me."

My pussy clenched at his words, so dirty.

I lifted one leg on either side of him and reached down to grip his cock, positioning him at my opening. I tried to ease down slow, torturing us both. But he gripped my hips and thrust up at the same time he shoved me down. I cried out in pleasure, watching him roll his head back against the couch, biting his lips.

He pushed me all the way down until his balls rested on my ass. We held ourselves there a moment, enjoying the feel of coming together again, knowing we did so on an equal playing field.

Coming together as two people who loved each other.

He lifted me to where just the tip of him rested inside me before plunging into me again. And again.

Over and over he fucked me harder, getting deeper. Sucking on my breasts, biting at my lips, swallowing up my groans of pleasure.

"Let me see your rub your clit." I did as I was told, letting my fingers slip over the bundle of nerves, barely hanging on. "I want to watch your hand working between us as I suck on your tits. I want to feel your pussy clenching me so tight, making me come inside your tight wet cunt."

It was too much. His words mixed with my fingers, the way he reached deeper each time, the feel of his tongue rolling around my nipples only to bite at them. It was too much, and in two more thrusts, I came. My head fell forward, and I moaned in his ear. My hands held on to his shoulders, feeling lost in the storm. But his fingers delved between us and he dragged out my orgasm with each swipe, with each thrust until he was groaning into my chest, holding himself inside me as he came.

I held him to my breast, his cool panting breaths sending chills across my sweaty skin. He kissed my chest and worked his way up my neck, nipping at my jaw before whispering in my ear. "I love you."

My smile could have lit up all of Cincinnati. The man I loved, seated deeply inside me, loved me in return.

What more could a girl ask for?

"Does this mean you'll hold my hand at Sunday brunch? Will you let me sit on your lap?"

He held me close, but pulled back with a wicked glint in his eye. "It may mean I get punched in the face again, but I would like nothing more than to claim you as mine for everyone to see."

"I love you." I wanted to say it over and over. Forever.

"I love you too." And I wanted to hear that over and over. Forever.

Epilogue

"Are you ready?"

"Yeah," Shane answered a little breathlessly. One hand still clenched the steering wheel, even though we'd been parked in Kings' parking lot for the last five minutes. The other was pretending to be relaxed in mine, where I let my thumb stroke the skin atop his hand.

"No matter what, I'm here for you. I love you."

He finally let go of the wheel and turned to me with a soft smile. "I love you, too."

I'd never tire of hearing it.

When I'd woken this morning, I decided not to bring up Sunday brunch. I wanted to dive right in and show the world that he was mine, but I worried it was too soon. I didn't want to push him.

Also, I kind of wanted a repeat of Saturday when he hadn't left the apartment at all. We scavenged his barren cabinets and refrigerator for enough sustenance to allow us to keep fucking like bunnies.

I couldn't have been more shocked when he was the one that rolled over, pulled me to his chest, and whispered, "Come to Sunday brunch with me."

I swallowed hard past the happy tears and easily agreed. I also gave him a long blow job to make sure he started the day with a positive explosion. Looking at him with his jaw clenched, swallowing nervously, I wondered if I should give him another one to calm him down.

"He'd be an idiot to let you go," I said. "And while I personally find him lacking in the brains department, I have faith he'll figure it out."

Shane leaned over and kissed me long and hard, sending chills all over my body.

As soon as we each rounded our sides of the car, we linked our hands back up and made our way into King's. Everyone was already sitting at the table and froze at our entrance, falling completely silent. My eyes sought out Jack as I gave Shane's hand a supportive squeeze and was met with flared nostrils and a snarling lip.

"You have a lot of nerve showing up here," Jack said, rising from his chair and taking angry strides toward Shane.

Before he could make it very far, I held up my free hand to halt his progress and gave him a fierce stare of my own.

"I love him. And he is part of this family. So you better love him too. He makes me happy. Period. The end."

"You go, Glen Coco!" Evie shouted from her position at the table.

"What?" Jack asked exasperatedly, jerking his head around toward her.

"Sorry. *Mean Girls* reference to cheer my girl on." She waved her hands in a rolling motion. "Proceed. But if you could forgive him soon, that'd be great because I'm starving."

Luella laughed as Jack turned back to glare at Shane. I turned to look at him to find nerves etched all over his face. His chest rose high before he let out a heavy sigh.

"Look, man. I'm sorry. I never meant for it to happen, but I'll never regret that it did. I love her."

Jack said nothing as he let Shane's words sink in.

I stepped into Shane's side, wrapping my arm around his waist, needing to be close after his proclamation.

"You ever hurt her, I will fucking murder you."

"Duly noted."

"Praise hands. Let's eat," Evie shouted.

I smiled up at Shane, and we moved to take a seat at the table. Jack continued to level dubious glares in Shane's direction, but quickly turned away when I whispered in Shane's ear and then nibbling my way down his neck.

"Ugh," Jack grunted.

"What?" I turned to Jack with raised eyebrows. "I've watched you and Lu all the time. Let's not even talk about the time I walked in on you and saw your pasty ass." I shuddered, and not for effect.

"Ahh, good memories." Evie smiled up at the ceiling like she was seeing it all over again. But when Jameson nudged her, a questioning look on his face, she stopped and gave him a peck. "But not as good as you, Jamie-boy."

"Or the time in the bathroom," Shane murmured under his breath.

"What?!" Jack and Luella's shocked voices asked in unison.

I leveled a death glare at Shane for even reminding me of that horrifying moment.

He just laughed and said, "Nothing," before leaning down to kiss me softly, erasing my irritation.

As everyone moved on talking about anything and everything, I curled into Shane's side, with our hands clasped tightly on top of the table for anyone to see.

This was my life. My family. And it was more than I ever could've imagined.

The End

Acknowledgements

As always, there is no way I could have done this without my family. My girls drive me to be better than I was yesterday and to be someone they can look up to. And my husband, my biggest supporter, the man that would move heaven and earth and sacrifice it all just to make me happy. I will never forget when I thought you were supposed to have gone back to base and I kept imagining how excited I'd be if I was wrong and you were at the party. It was all my imagination, right? But there you were, waiting for me so we could rock this world together! I love you.

Karla, the only woman who can make me ridiculously happy and also make me want to plot her death. Haha! I couldn't make these books what they are without you asking the hard questions. The ones that really suck and are hard to answer. But they make the book something I can be confident in. Your friendship gives me life and I couldn't survive without our endlessly rambling voice messages. I love you.

Rachel and Georgeanna, my ride or die sisters. I wouldn't survive life without you ladies by my side. I cherish our day drinking adventures and late night get togethers, full of laughter and the best support a woman can ask for. I love you both so much and hope to God that the Army never separates us. Even if it does, I know no distance will keep us apart.

Becca, my champion. My goodness I have never had anyone believe in me quite like you do. I never would have made it as far as I have without you forcing my book on everyone. Without the support and care only you are capable of with your amazing heart, I'd never be where I am now. God blessed me when He placed you in my life.

To Linda, from Foreword PR. Oh my goodness, you have become so important to me. I couldn't imagine any of the success I've stumbled upon without your help. You were so amazing to take me under your wing and guide me through this. Thank you for taking me on, and thank you for being so amazing and kind.

To my amazing beta readers. Serena, your messages and GIFs were everything. I love that you loved Shane so much and took a chance on reading Imagine Me. Your feedback was perfectly on point. Thank you! Julia, I'm forever grateful that you took the time to message me. You gave me such perfect feedback that really made me think about Shane and Juliana's story. I couldn't have done it without you. I will await the day that we can finally meet and ramble awkwardly together in person! Haha! #RamblersUnite

Karen, there are no words for how grateful I am for your editing. It is thorough and lets me feel confident about how clean it is. I hope to keep you forever because I can't imagine ever putting another book out without your talented eyes on it. Thank you!

Alexis, my go to proofreader. I love your honest feedback and always trust your comments. I could never not have faith in someone who loves Original Sinners just as much as I do! I'm so glad we connected. You have been more than just a proofreader to me, you have guided me through this community and always supported me. Thank you for being my friend.

Najla Qambar, you are by far the most talented cover designer ever. How can you not be when I only send you vague answers and complete indecisiveness? And yet, there you are, making the cover I couldn't even imagine. They are always gorgeous and everything I could want.

To all the awesome ladies in my reader group. I love talking music with you and your feedback on excerpts and teasers give me the fire I need to continue. Thank you for all you support and faith in me.

To all the author, readers, bloggers, and bookstagrammers. I have to fight the urge to list all of you off because you all just blow me away. Every time I get a chance to talk to an author or they share something of mine, I'm floored. I'm in so much shock that you can even see me. Haha! I will mention Sierra Simone, because you may not know this, but when you messaged me about Shame Me Not, I was in tears of joy. I was so honored by your comments. Especially from someone who writes ridiculously sexy as hell sex scenes. Whew! Thank you for taking the time. I'm forever grateful.

Bloggers and bookstagrammers, I would be nothing without you. Literally. You spread the word, you take time out of your busy lives and share my work just out of your passion for reading. Your pictures are gorgeous and your words are kind. You make this community go around and I see every post and share, and I love all of them.

Readers, you are the most phenomenal people and I'm always humbled by all your feedback. Every time someone messages me about a book, I am blown away. I know how hard it is to reach out and possibly not get a response, and you do it anyway. I have loved and reread every single message. Thank you for taking a chance on my stories. There are so many amazing books and never enough time to read them, so I'm so happy that you picked up one of mine. Thank you, thank you, thank you!

About Fiona Cole

Fiona Cole is a military wife and a stay at home mom with degrees in biology and chemistry. As much as she loved science, she decided to postpone her career to stay at home with her two little girls, and immersed herself in the world of books until finally deciding to write her own.

Fiona loves hearing from her readers, so be sure to follow her on social media.

Facebook: www.facebook.com/authorfionacole
Instagram, Pinterest, & Twitter: @authorfionacole
Email: authorfionacole@gmail.com
Newsletter: http://eepurl.com/bEvHtL
Reader Group: Books, Wine, and Music with Fiona Cole
Amazon
BookBub
Book + Main

Other books by Fiona Cole

All books are free on Kindle Unlimited

Where You Can Find Me

Deny Me

Shame (Shame Me Not #1)

Make It to the Altar (Shame Me Not #1.5)

Made in the USA
Monee, IL
17 July 2022